A DEATH AT
CAMP DAVID

Barry Zeilman

A DEATH AT CAMP DAVID

A NOVEL

HARRY A. MILMAN

Library of Congress Control Number:		2015918318
ISBN:	Hardcover	978-1-5144-2317-2
	Softcover	978-1-5144-2319-6
	eBook	978-1-5144-2318-9

Print information available on the last page.

Rev. date: 11/06/2015

To order additional copies of this book, contact:
Xlibris
1-888-795-4274
www.Xlibris.com
Orders@Xlibris.com
726950

To Kyra, Tyce, Jeremy, and Emily, with love

Acknowledgments

My sincere gratitude to Laurie Gilkenson for her hard work, helpful suggestions, and careful editing of the manuscript.

My heartfelt thanks to Jennifer McGinn for her excellent photography, invaluable time, and utmost patience.

Chapter 1

AN UNUSUALLY LONG heat wave engulfed the United States, and there was no respite in sight. All across the nation, record temperatures were being set. In Minnesota, residents who were accustomed to seeing their temperatures fall in the dead of winter to an average of twenty degrees below zero, sometimes reaching as low as forty below, saw their thermometers register over ninety degrees. "But it is a dry heat," they would often hear said. Dry or not, it was hotter than deer at the height of mating season.

Nevada was warmer than at any time since the 1950s when mushroom clouds filled the night skies as the state became a testing ground for nuclear warheads. Toxic clouds became a tourist attraction that was visible from as far away as one hundred miles and from many of the windows of major hotels in downtown Las Vegas. Those who viewed the showering inferno eventually paid for it as cancer and other diseases were inflicted upon them by the radiation and toxic fumes to which they were exposed.

Florida, which normally sees the departure of its snowbirds by Easter, experienced an increase in its population as the birds returned to roost, looking to escape the uncharacteristic and escalating temperatures they found in their northern habitat. "Come on down" was more than a sales pitch by Floridian real estate agents. It became a rallying cry for those escaping the overheated North. At least in Florida, cool waves of the Atlantic Ocean and wide open spaces kept temperatures lower than in the congested and overpopulated Northeast.

The question on everyone's mind was, was this a sign of climate change? Some had doubt, believing that extremes in weather conditions were part of the normal cycle of the universe. After all, hadn't the ice age occurred at a time when there were no man-made carbon emissions?

Environmental scientists researched climate change and global warming for decades, but the public was alerted to its potential problems in 2006. It was then that the documentary film *An Inconvenient Truth*, directed by Davis Guggenheim, about the efforts of former vice president of the United States Al Gore to educate citizens about the phenomenon was released. Although he lost the presidential election in 2000 after a controversial ending to a hard-fought political campaign, Gore managed to win the hearts and minds of the electorate both with his farewell speech and his dedication and need to enlighten the public about environmental catastrophes that loomed if climate change was not taken seriously. Now, in large part because of Gore's awakening of the public's consciousness, any reports of melting arctic ice or havoc caused to the environment by rising temperatures, such as forest fires and tornadoes, inevitably took center stage on the evening news.

Thus, it followed that with a heat wave of this magnitude blanketing the nation, many of its citizens concluded that climate change undoubtedly was the root cause of the elevated temperatures that were sweeping the country.

In the Big Easy, where people take a hot and muggy summer night in stride, like a horse suffering with the buzzing of flies around its head, the heat wave was unbearable mainly for its duration, for it was hotter and longer than in anyone's recent memory. Temperatures were above one hundred degrees Fahrenheit for the longest time, and the humidity hovered at over 90 percent. The air was denser than molasses on a hot summer's day, so thick and heavy with moisture that one could seemingly cut it with a knife yet never dull the blade. The warm, stagnant embrace was as inviting as honeybees lured by the sight of maple syrup. It was absolutely stifling and, by any measure, excruciatingly hot and humid.

It was against this backdrop of heat and humidity on an otherwise uneventful night in July, a night in which air conditioning was at a premium and stray dogs looked for any available shade, that Officer Gonzalez walked his beat on Bourbon Street and its intersecting alleys in the wee hours of the morning in New Orleans's famous, some would dare say infamous, French Quarter.

Officer David Gonzalez was a longtime member of the New Orleans Police Department (NOPD), of which Hispanics comprised only 2 percent of the workforce. The city is divided into nine police districts, each of which is headed by a police commander. Officer Gonzalez's beat in the French Quarter was in the Eighth District.

His mother, who was very religious, named Gonzalez after a king, thinking that a regal name would bring him good luck. It did not always turn out that way. When Gonzalez was a teenager, his friends teased him and called him the Hispanic Jew, mainly because besides being named after a Jewish king, he often played with

Jewish kids. Occasionally, he would see his former classmates as grown men, only now he would be on the freedom side of prison bars while they would be on the other.

As he walked, cognizant of the nearly deserted streets, Gonzalez passed Preservation Hall, where New Orleans jazz played since 1961. Occasionally, he checked locks and bolts on gates and doors of local establishments, ensuring that they were closed and burglary proof.

Off in the distance, Gonzalez saw a car parked by the side of the road that was rocking from side to side. He hastened his pace toward the car, which was nearly a block away. "What is that all about?" he wondered.

Gonzalez walked toward the automobile, approaching it from behind, concerned about his safety, which was paramount. He did not plan to disappoint his wife, who depended on him to be home in the morning when his shift was over, arriving just in time to kiss his children good-bye as they hurried off to school. Gonzalez was a family man, and his family was his prized possession. He would not do anything that would jeopardize his safety and leave his wife a widow and his children fatherless. He planned to take care of his family's needs, and a retirement pension was still more than ten years away.

But this was New Orleans, and Gonzalez understood that anything could happen at any time in this section of town, as it did during Katrina in the final days of August 2005 when turmoil and mayhem were rampant. He would sooner forget those early days in his career. It was not a good time for the NOPD. There was looting, there were killings, there was all-out lawlessness.

Although at the time, *Law and Order*, a program created for television by Dick Wolf, garnered a number of Emmy Awards, law and order was not to be found in New Orleans in the aftermath of Katrina. There were reports that over two hundred NOPD officers deserted the city during the storm. Newspapers described the city as Dodge of old, where people took the law into their own hands simply because they could. It was alleged that the NOPD covered up crimes that were committed by some of its own officers at the height of the storm. Gone was the vibrant community where Mardi Gras was celebrated by people of all persuasions and ethnicity.

"Why is it," Gonzalez pondered as he walked toward the waiting car, "that at the slightest opportunity, people revert to their animalistic selves, and everything that they learned from the good book about 'love thy neighbor' evaporates into thin air? People," he concluded, "are a pain in the ass."

"Give me a dog anytime," he lamented. "They love you, they keep you warm, and they never complain."

As he walked, Gonzalez recalled that the famous comedian Jerry Seinfeld joked that if a Martian landed at the exact moment when you walked your dog and saw you picking up poop, he would get the wrong impression about who was the master. "That may be true," Gonzalez reflected, "or maybe he will actually get the right idea. After all, sometimes humans act like animals. Take *Planet of the Apes* as a case in point. Now, that was a great movie. They don't make them like that anymore."

Gonzalez was almost within earshot of the car, and he saw that he was not wrong. It definitely was rocking. No doubt about it. Although the streetlight nearby was not lit and it was fairly dark, he was able to identify the car as a late-model Lexus four-door sedan. In the pitch of night, it was difficult to tell whether the car was blue, black, or maroon.

Although he did not feel threatened yet, Gonzalez unbuckled his holster just in case he needed to reach for his weapon. To his surprise, he saw that all four doors of the vehicle were closed although he could not tell if they were locked, and the windows were rolled all the way up.

"I hope the air conditioning is running," he muttered under his breath.

Now, only a few steps away, Gonzalez saw that the car's rear window was fogged from the steam being generated within. From that distance, he had difficulty looking into the car. He thought that he would be able to get a better peek through one of its windows once he was closer. "Someone or something must be inside and moving about," he concluded.

The motor was running, which meant that the air conditioning most likely was operating. A person or persons were in the car, but what they were doing there Gonzalez did not know.

Looking through the rear window of the car whose dashboard light faintly glowed, he saw a man seated in the rear wearing a fedora that was too big for his head, obscuring his face as it fell slightly over his forehead, covering his eyebrows. The man wore a dark jacket, perhaps a blue blazer, and was hunched over something that Gonzalez could not readily identify. There was gray hair protruding at the back of the man's neck, below the fedora, and Gonzalez guessed that the man probably was in his late fifties. His hands were wrapped around something large, and he appeared to be struggling. The more he struggled, the more the car shook.

About to remove his gun from its holster, but just before doing so, Gonzalez realized that the man in the car was not struggling but, instead, was involved in a highly charged embrace with a young woman. Their passion escalated to climactic heights the likes of which often are seen in movies but which Gonzalez rarely saw as he patrolled his beat in the French Quarter. Slowly, the couple moved to the rhythm of the night, their lips pressing against one another, unable or unwilling to part. It was clear that the man was being seduced with great delight and experience by a voluptuous woman of substantial beauty, who was in her thirties.

Her hair was bleached blond, a color that would have made Marilyn Monroe envious. Gonzalez couldn't tell the color of her eyes for they were tightly shut. Her ruby lips were locked on the man's mouth as her hands methodically roamed his body, attempting to remove his shirt and tie and unzip his pants.

The man with the fedora was frantically trying to unsnap the woman's blouse with fingers that were so thick it would have been a miracle had he been able to do so. This steamy sight was very much in keeping with the overly heated night in the Big Easy. Gonzalez was not a Peeping Tom, however, so he diverted his eyes from the sexually charged scene.

The pair of lovers were entranced, and they did not notice that Gonzalez was nearby, separated from their inner sanctum only by glass and steel. Their passionate, long embrace would have made Adam and Eve proud. Anthony and Cleopatra, whose liaisons during their turbulent years together as they sailed the Nile is legendary among historians of the period, would have found no fault in the intertwining of their bodies.

The woman's smooth, rounded, firm breasts rested tightly against the man's chest, and her kisses awakened his manhood, which she felt with great delight against her abdomen. This made her kiss him even more passionately and with greater verve, which aroused him even further. Such passion was not felt between two bodies since Richard Burton made love to Elizabeth Taylor.

Their fingers explored their respective bodies, leaving no crevice untouched. They marveled at providing each other pleasure while receiving pleasure in return. With each kiss, the man with the fedora gently stroked her inner being, ensuring that she was as satisfied as he was. Thus, pleasure was given in the heat and humidity of the Big Easy, and even greater pleasure was received.

Determined not to disturb the couple, at least not just yet, Gonzalez decided to let them enjoy their rendezvous with ecstasy for a little while longer. It would be unfair to interrupt them at the height of imminent pleasure. He figured that he only had to wait a minute or two more before her moaning and the man's groaning would subside, at which time he would apprehend them for loitering.

So as the man with the fedora and the woman with the bleached blond hair continued their escalating passion, Gonzalez stood by the side of the car, hidden from view by the darkness of the streetlamp, patiently waiting for their passion to reach orgasmic proportions then to dissipate in exhaustion.

And when the woman finally let out a loud moan and the man with the fedora heaved a long sigh of contentment, only then did the Lexus come to a restful stop. It was at that moment that Gonzalez knocked loudly on the driver's rear window, startling the pair of lovers.

Chapter 2

"WHO THE HELL is that?"

The car's engine was still running, so the man with the fedora pressed a button on the side of the door to electronically lower the window as he zipped up his trousers, leaving one of his shirttails dangling out of his pants and his belt unbuckled.

"Oh, it's you, Dr. Kramer," Gonzalez answered, not expecting to recognize any of the car's occupants. "I didn't know you were in town."

"Hello, Gonzalez." Kramer resumed dressing, tucking his shirttails back into his pants and buckling his belt.

Dr. Bob Kramer always called Officer Gonzalez by his last name. He has known Gonzalez for many years, having seen him as a witness at trials in which he had also testified. These were usually DUI cases, or cases of assault in which the use of alcohol or illicit drugs was implicated.

"I see you're busy. I didn't mean to disturb you. I will just say good night." Gonzalez began walking away.

"Good night, Gonzalez. Say hello to your lovely wife and kids!" Kramer shouted out the side window at the image of the officer as it faded from view.

Kramer was a forensic toxicologist who testified about the harmful effects of drugs. As a toxicology expert, he reviewed the scientific facts of a case and provided a plausible explanation to link a toxic effect, including death, to ingestion of a drug, often when taken in large amounts.

People often asked him how to become an expert witness. "First, you become an expert, then you become an expert witness," he would reply.

Kramer had a PhD in pharmacology, a biological science dealing with drugs and their therapeutic effects on the body, but his extensive experience was in toxicology, a science that deals with the harmful effects of drugs and chemicals. He was very good at what he did as he was able to communicate scientific information in an easily understandable manner and to connect with a jury. That was not only a gift, it was an art. It was for that reason that Kramer was often called by print and electronic media to provide his expert opinion on toxicology issues or for on-air interviews at local radio and television news programs.

Kramer thought of himself as debonair and suave, modeling himself after Sean Connery and the original James Bond rather than the bumbling Chief Inspector Clouseau of *Pink Panther* fame. He wore Italian suits and shirts that were tailor-made for him by Kiton, an Italian manufacturer based in Naples, and he favored Ferragamo shoes. Unfortunately for Kramer, no matter how well dressed he was, he was no Sean Connery. Kramer was short, only five feet five inches tall, in his late fifties, and had a slight paunch around his midriff. Although pleasant enough, he had a small dark mustache that was not very becoming. He wore black-rimmed glasses that were too big for his face, and he had a receding hairline that had receded as far back as it could go. He was left with what some people would refer to as a "parting of the seas"—a vast arid expanse in the middle of the head with graying hair all around the perimeter. At least he never had to worry about where to part his hair.

Not particularly religious, he was brought up in a home where Yiddish was spoken. Although his mother was Jewish, his father was gentile, which made for some interesting conversations around the kitchen table. Some Yiddish words still entered Kramer's vocabulary. He liked to joke that whenever he went to confession, he would bring a lawyer. Women flocked to him in spite of his less than stunning physical appearance because of his intellect and charm, both of which made him exude with confidence.

After rolling up his window, Kramer glanced quizzically at the woman sitting next to him. She was busy looking in a mirror while putting on her lipstick and combing her long blond hair that got disheveled by the frenetic activity in which they had indulged only moments earlier. Her navy-colored suit had wrinkled, but she did not seem to mind. Her Christian Louboutin open-toe navy pumps lay on the floor by her feet, and she scrambled to put them back on.

Joanne Marie Johnson was a petite, slender, and a rather attractive hotshot attorney in her midthirties. She recently joined the Orleans Parish Public Defender's Office after working at a high-powered law firm because, "Only if I get down in the gutter can I understand why people commit white-collar crime."

Aside from her intellect, which was considerable, Johnson had two other attributes that were easily appreciated in court. She was well endowed. But what made Johnson's breasts so spectacular was not their size, which was considerable and optimal, but their uniformity, roundness, and firmness, which made them so sumptuous that they would have given Anna Nicole Smith a substantial run for her money had she been alive. It was this advantage over her male opponents that gave Johnson an edge with both men on a jury and most judges and helped her win cases that sometimes had little merit.

Johnson was a shiksa, a woman who is not of the Jewish faith, of which Kramer's mother would not have approved. But Kramer was not interested in a committed relationship. He was only interested in Johnson's breasts. He got more than he bargained for in the backseat of his rented Lexus. Things were not always easy in the Big Easy, but Johnson was.

They just concluded a three-day trial in which the defendant was accused of assault. He was charged with severely beating a woman with a board while under the influence of alcohol. Johnson was assigned to the case, and she immediately contacted Kramer to be her expert. They worked together on and off in the past, and this case required Kramer's expertise in alcohol intoxication.

Kramer was reluctant to travel to Louisiana for what was to be a fairly straightforward case. But he liked working under Johnson and would have liked it even more if Johnson worked under him in a downtown hotel room. The thought of seeing her again was enough to get his juices flowing, so he agreed to assist in the case.

At trial, evidence was presented that the defendant and the female victim drank several beers together and began arguing. Eventually, the defendant hit the woman across the head with a board. Police arrived about thirty minutes after the assault and took the victim, who had severe bruises on her head, and the defendant, who had lacerations across his arms and face, to an emergency room where his blood alcohol concentration, or BAC, at 0.27, was more than three times the legal limit, and hers was 0.18.

Under questioning, Kramer described for the jury the various physiological effects that alcohol can cause, including cognitive and psychomotor deficits. He pointed out that impairment begins with the first drink. At a BAC as low as 0.02, there is marked relaxation, reduced ability to display good judgment, decreased reaction times and alertness, divided attention deficits, and decreased inhibition. In addition, Kramer noted that symptoms of alcohol intoxication increase in severity with increasing intake of alcohol so that by a BAC of 0.18 to 0.27, there is great impairment of many physiological, cognitive, and psychomotor skills.

It took Kramer all his energy to focus on the questions Johnson posed as she paraded her assets in front of him. She slowly led him to admit that not only was the defendant impaired by alcohol, but so was his female companion. Moreover, the victim contributed to the altercation that ultimately resulted in her injuries and was not an innocent bystander.

As he observed Johnson in action, Kramer thought that she was magnificent. He slowly followed her with his eyes, all the while trying to appear professional and not be distracted by her extraordinary silhouette. His mind, however, painted a vision of Johnson sitting naked with her legs crossed at his bedside, holding a book that partially covered her bosom, her face tilting downward but her eyes looking upward ever so slightly in his direction.

Cross-examining the witnesses, Johnson sensed Kramer's eyes surveying her body, and she liked it. She was hankering for him for some time, but the opportunity never arose.

"Today is the day," she decided.

It did not take long for the jury to arrive at a verdict—guilty of aggravated assault with extenuating circumstances. The defendant received a reduced sentence. It was a victory as far as Johnson and Kramer were concerned.

When the trial was over, Kramer offered to take Johnson to dinner to celebrate their victory. He arranged for a late-night reservation. They chatted as they ate and drank wine, all the while glancing into each other's eyes across the table, occasionally brushing their knees against one another. Body language was everything, but dessert was something else. They were not going to have it at the restaurant. Kramer had other plans for a sweet ending to their day.

They finished dinner close to midnight and strolled the French Quarter, marveling at the sound of music flowing from bars that lined both sides of Bourbon Street. The quarter was fairly empty because of the heat, and by half past one in the morning, they reached Kramer's parked Lexus. When he opened the front passenger door to let Johnson in, she motioned him to the backseat. It was time to get his just desserts, but food was not on her mind. And as Kramer concentrated on enjoying the quality and quantity of his portion, Officer Gonzalez knocked on the car window at a very inopportune moment.

It was nearly three in the morning by the time Kramer rolled into bed. He barely fell asleep when his phone rang. It was six o'clock.

"Hello," he mumbled into the mouthpiece, hardly awake.

"Dr. Kramer, you better get over here." It was Trudy calling from his office in the Maryland suburbs.

"Why, what is going on?" It was seven in the morning on the East Coast. *An ungodly hour to be calling, but it must be important if she is calling so early*, Kramer thought.

"They found a body."

"Where?" He did not understand the urgency of the call.

"Camp David."

Kramer paused, trying to shake the cobwebs out of his head and to comprehend what Trudy was saying.

"Yes, that Camp David," she added. "You better get over here. Now!"

"Oy vey."

Chapter 3

IT WAS FOUR years earlier that the Democrats felt they had the best chance of regaining political power after a dismal eight years of Republican rule. The country was tired of all the bickering and the policies of a Republican administration. It was time to clean house.

The party's nominee for president of the United States was Leslie Breckenridge, a seasoned politician from Texas who was rarely seen without his favorite cigar resting between his pointer and middle fingers. He never lit it, but its presence, he often said, was a reminder of the number of years since he quit smoking, now nearing twenty.

Breckenridge was a big man, standing six feet five inches tall. His Texas drawl and long silvery hair gave him a distinguished appearance, similar to that of a world-renowned physician or a learned academic. His many years in political life helped him learn how to capitalize on his charm and experience and how to cajole recalcitrant congressional colleagues so that they would come around to his point of view. They never failed him. That he was well liked by his peers and, more importantly, by fellow Americans made him the obvious choice that year as the Democratic Party's nominee for president.

With his finger on the pulse of the voters, Breckenridge felt that the time was ripe for Democrats to again make history. He decided to choose a woman to join him on the ticket and selected Jessica Elizabeth Worthing as his vice presidential running mate.

The first time a woman was nominated to a top spot on the Democratic ticket was in 1984 when former vice president and presidential candidate Walter Mondale selected Geraldine Ferraro to join him. Unfortunately, they did not win the general election. Then, in 2008, Hillary Clinton ran in the primaries to become her party's nominee for president. She was the nation's First Lady during her husband's two terms as president and was an elected senator from New York. It was a very close primary, but Clinton did not win the Democratic nomination. Nevertheless, the party made history that year by nominating the first African American candidate, Barack Obama, for president. He easily beat his Republican challenger, John McCain, in the general election.

Jessica Worthing was an excellent choice for vice president. She was a very experienced and seasoned politician who was married to John Worthing, a wildly successful CEO of an Internet company. Although they had no children, the Worthings were a power couple in Washington political circles and were invited to all the most important social events. That they made a handsome duo was a definite plus.

With one term in the house and two terms as senator from California with a strong congressional record for getting things done, Worthing's selection was applauded by Democrats. Unlike Sarah Palin, who was the Republican contender for vice president with John McCain, Worthing was attractive but not disarmingly so, and she was extremely smart. In addition, while Palin allegedly claimed that she could see Russia from her kitchen window, Worthing actually visited Russia on various diplomatic missions as a representative of the United States government. It was not a coincidence that she was known as Worthy Worthing. When she spoke, the people definitely listened.

Jessica Elizabeth Littleton first met John Worthing when they were both undergraduate students at Duke University. They took a philosophy class together and soon found that they had similar interests and aspirations. Both were extremely ambitious with type-A personalities. Both were extroverts, well liked, and with many friends. But unbeknownst to others, both were gay. Although they kept their sexual orientation a tightly held secret, hidden from everyone including their closest friends and confidants, their sexual preference was what brought them together, and their secret was the glue that kept their marriage going for more than fifteen years.

Society now was more tolerant of gays than it was in the 1950s, but Littleton and Worthing felt that if they wanted to advance in their chosen professions, Littleton in politics and Worthing in business, they had to keep their sexual preference a secret. Littleton was mindful that there were only six openly gay members in the history of Congress. Barney Frank was the most prominent and Tammy Baldwin the only openly lesbian congresswoman who was also elected in 2012 as the first openly lesbian member of the Senate. However, there was never an openly gay person in the White House. John Worthing was likewise aware that the majority of

CEOs of Fortune 500 companies were heterosexual and that it would be much easier for him to advance in the business world if he was perceived as straight.

Littleton and Worthing understood that being single and gay, let alone openly gay, would limit them professionally, more so in the upper reaches of politics than in the boardrooms of big business. They concluded that marriage was the best way to maintain their hidden sexuality and to appear as successful heterosexuals in public. Obviously, the marriage would not be consummated, but having no children would not be a problem. People would think that they were a couple who were focused on their careers with no time to raise a family. After considering all the possible pitfalls and obstacles that they would face, they decided to marry. It was to be a marriage of convenience.

After finishing Harvard Law School, and with her eyes set on being elected to Congress, Jessica Worthing first had a stint in state politics and then was elected to Congress where she served in both houses. Along with her good looks, intellect, and hard work, she was on her way to a position of leadership in the Democratic Party. She was confident that she made the right decision to keep her secret safe by marrying John Worthing. Besides, she truly liked him even though their marriage was asexual.

Unlike his wife, John Worthing chose to make his mark in the booming Internet industry, where growth and opportunity were to be found everywhere. He obtained his MBA at Harvard and began a succession of Internet companies. The first company he founded placed part-time job seekers with potential employers in the service sector. After selling the company, he formed an Internet florist followed by an Internet greeting-card company and, finally, his most lucrative company of all, an Internet insurance company that specialized in long-term care and financial services. When he sold his shares in the company, he was forty-eight years old and worth 150 million dollars. It was time for a new venture. He chose to form an Internet company that brought glamour and style to middle-class women of all means by selling designer seconds—designer clothes with minor imperfections and ones that were previously worn. Financial success followed him again.

As undergraduates, the Worthings took acting classes with the express purpose of learning how to project an image that was different from their own. What they learned came in handy as they rose in the ranks of their chosen professions. But while they appeared to be successful heterosexuals, the Worthings were, in fact, frustrated gays who sneaked about in the shadows to satisfy their sexual appetites.

They took great care to maintain their discretion and to avoid professional calamity when gratifying their sexual desires, finding outlets that did not jeopardize or compromise their professional standings. No one suspected the Worthings of sexual indiscretions. They vacationed at popular tourist spots around the globe, such as in Amsterdam, at Super Paradise Beach on the island of Mykonos, or in Sweden, where there were ample tourist sights to behold and, coincidentally, where the gay population was plentiful. These dream vacations were far from the glaring eyes of the American press and ensured anonymity. They were filled with sightseeing and sufficient sexual activity to last the Worthings until their next vacation. When they returned from their travels, the Worthings would be refreshed, sexually rejuvenated, and ready to tackle new professional challenges. They relished their vacations, looking forward to the next one with great anticipation.

Chapter 4

THE BRECKENRIDGE-WORTHING DEMOCRATIC ticket was enthusiastically embraced by the electorate, and nearly every state in the nation voted them in. It was a landslide. The mood of the country shifted back toward middle-class values, and the Democrats swept the White House and both chambers of Congress. But as sweet as the victory was, it did not come without a price. The Democrats made significant concessions to avoid gridlock. Several of the chairmanships of important congressional committees were given to Republicans, and the newly elected Democratic president appointed two Republicans to key posts in his cabinet.

The first year of the Breckenridge-Worthing administration went fairly smoothly. The political honeymoon was long and productive. The country was back on its feet as employment improved. The nation was at peace, and the economy was humming along. As vice president, Worthing was not threatening to the Republicans. She presided over the Senate, provided counsel to the president, and attended funerals. The press sometimes dubbed her the Second First Lady. She was seen but not heard, which was fine with the Republicans.

When Jessica Worthing became vice president of the United States the Worthings lost much of the freedom of sexual exploration that they enjoyed when she was in Congress. No longer were they able to move about at leisure, their every move being accompanied by an entourage of secret service personnel and assorted political staff. The vice president was a strong-willed woman who was able to contain her sexual cravings and avoid impropriety. Her husband, however, had difficulty keeping his sexual needs under control. Nevertheless, he was smart enough to know that if he acted on his sexual urges indiscriminately and was caught, it would be the end of both of their careers, which would be too great a price to pay for sexual gratification. Rather than lose everything that they built together, John Worthing stewed in his inability to fulfill his sexual desires while his wife maintained her stalwart demeanor. This inevitably caused strife and resentment in their marriage and put a wedge in their relationship that resulted in frequent verbal blowups behind closed doors.

It would not be long before John Worthing could no longer contain himself and he began letting his frustrated penis rather than his substantial intellect dictate his actions. His sexual exploits were fraught with personal and political danger, but he managed to keep them to a minimum. He continued to walk the tightrope between societal expectations and his sexual urges, but like any addict, his sexual appetite required frequent feeding. There was an element of danger associated with his sexual exploits that stimulated his sexual desire even further. This was of great concern to his wife, who counted on him to adhere to the pact they made when they married.

Then suddenly, early in the eighteenth month of his first term as president, Breckenridge died after suffering an unexpected episode of aortic dissection. The condition, which comes on quickly and without warning, is an abnormal separation of tissues within the walls of the aorta, one of the largest blood vessels in the body. It can be caused by high blood pressure, family history of the condition, disease of connective tissue, or severe trauma to the chest, and is almost always impossible to diagnose. John Ritter, a popular TV star of an earlier era, died from this condition in 2003.

With Breckenridge's death, Jessica Worthing assumed the awesome responsibilities of president of the United States. History was made once again. Her husband, however, simmered, knowing that his personal life would be scrutinized even more closely, now that his wife was president. There was no way for them to get back to the anonymity they once enjoyed. He felt trapped. The irony that as a closeted gay man, he would be jokingly referred to as the First Lady did not escape him.

One of the early decisions Jessica Worthing had to make after she was sworn in as president was to choose a vice president, under the terms of the Twenty-Fifth Amendment, who would be ready to take on the presidency in the event that she was unable to do so. Not since Nixon appointed Gerald Ford in 1973 to be the fortieth vice president after Spiro Agnew resigned was the American government placed in such a predicament. Although several potential candidates in the Democratic Party could have easily filled the position, Worthing was astutely aware of the backlash within the Republican Party toward her becoming president. First, she was not elected to the presidency yet held the highest office in the land, and second, she was a woman and a Democrat at that. It would have been hellish for her during the remaining two years of Breckenridge's term if she was not careful in her selection of a vice president.

Rising to the challenge and in a move of extreme courage, Worthing chose Eric Bunting, a Republican, to be her vice president. Only fifty-seven years of age, Bunting had all the right credentials to advance in politics. He came to Congress after cutting his political teeth in Minnesota, where as governor, he instituted laws that provided for taxation of proceeds earned by gambling casinos located on Native American reservations. As a Republican congressman, he was able to compromise with fellow Democrats and get laws passed that were beneficial to business while, at the same time, avoiding alienating the members of the Tea Party, who were wielding enormous political power. This was very difficult to do, but Bunting managed to do it and, as a result, accumulated many political friends. That he never married and was handsome and athletic added to his glamour, mystery, and style. He was always sought after as a chaperon for female celebrities and TV personalities. As vice president, his stature would be further enhanced to heights that even he could not have envisioned.

The selection of Bunting surprised everybody, including Republicans. It resonated well with the voters, however, and signaled that here was a woman president of courage, determination, and conviction who was ready to make tough decisions and tackle problems head-on with strength and fortitude. As a moderate, Bunting was rapidly confirmed by Congress, and he became the new vice president to stand alongside a Democratic president for the good of the country. It was unprecedented.

The Worthing-Bunting alliance worked pretty well during their first year together. Congress was determined to show political unity, and the Democrats and the Republicans returned to the cozy days of attending functions together at the National Press Club and to fine dining at Capitol Hill restaurants where they imbibed and conducted back room politics that soon became the norm.

In the third year of Breckenridge's term, it was time to begin thinking about Worthing's election to her first full term as president of the United States in her own right. Within Worthing's inner circle, questions arose whether Bunting should be kept on the ticket. Many thought that selecting a Republican for vice president was a bold decision that helped Worthing move the country forward after Breckenridge's unexpected death. However, a year later, the country was nearly fully recovered from the shock and having Bunting, a

Republican, on the Democratic ticket might now be a liability.

What especially irked the president and gave her pause was that Bunting was a loose cannon. Although very savvy politically, he was a bachelor who enjoyed being photographed with aspiring young starlets in sometimes overexuberant and slightly inebriated condition, often with a can of his favorite beer in hand. His indiscretions, which he seemed to ignore, reflected badly on the administration. However, his close relationship with the Republican establishment and the Tea Party, which grew in power and influence since the days of President Obama, made it difficult to remove him from the ticket.

The Democratic primary season was fairly dull with no viable challengers to Worthing and Bunting on the horizon. No Democrat with real or perceived aspiration for the presidency was willing to challenge the incumbent for the nomination. All felt that the Worthing-Bunting ticket had too much going for it and would be unbeatable.

Unlike the Democrats, however, who had their candidates for president and vice president well secured, the Republican Party had no presumptive candidate for president. The field of likely candidates was limited, and very few eligible Republicans were willing to run against a Democrat who had a Republican as her running mate. What would their slogan be? "Vote for a Republican and change the country"? Most decided to sit out the election and to watch the unfolding campaigns from their easy chairs in front of their television sets.

For many Republicans, it appeared that no matter which party succeeded in winning the White House, one of their own would help lead the country either as vice president, if the Democrats won, or as president, if the Republicans won. The party, however, was in dire straits as it had to nominate candidates for president and vice president, if only to give the impression of providing the electorate a choice between two distinctly different governing philosophies.

Chapter 5

A NEWCOMER TO elected office, Danford Slocum was a right of center Republican with a long history of working on the fringes of public policy. Never elected to high office, he was a successful business tycoon with bad hair and an economics background who worked behind the scenes and challenged politicians to pass legislation that would benefit business initiatives. There were rumors that money and other favors exchanged hands, including occasional rendezvous with call girls, but this was never substantiated. He was financially successful and had a way in political circles that made him an attractive potential presidential nominee. A rugged jaw and a ready smile were an added bonus.

While Worthing was in politics for nearly twenty years and had her political machinery in place, Slocum had to scramble to catch up if he wanted to be the Republican nominee for president. Established Republican politicians offered their political apparatus and advice, but he would have none of it. Having spent his entire professional life in finance, he knew that past performance was no guarantee of future success. His political team would be built from scratch with young, innovative, and hungry political entrepreneurs who were complimented with a few, selectively chosen political gurus. He knew that only by thinking outside the box would he have a chance of beating Worthing in the general election. He thought long and hard and decided to consult George Tewkesbury, one of the few people he trusted.

Slocum and Tewkesbury were longtime friends since their days together in Afghanistan. They fought side by side and saved each other's lives more often than a dog could wag his tail. Tewkesbury returned from Afghanistan suffering from depression. Extremely introverted and reserved, and after serving in Afghanistan also clinically depressed, he spent his days escaping with pharmaceuticals, doctors, and psychiatric clinics. Slocum, on the other hand, put his war experiences behind him and backpacked through Europe for six months. Eventually, he became successful in business while Tewkesbury learned to control his mood swings with antipsychotic medication and began a career consulting for a firm that conducted polls.

In due course, Tewkesbury formed his own firm, Tewkesbury Associates, focusing mostly on polling for politicians and companies who leaned right of center. Slocum used Tewkesbury's services on many occasions to help him decide where the likelihood for financial success lay among several potential investments.

Over the years, Slocum and Tewkesbury became more than friends. They became buddies, liking each other as brothers and consulting each other for advice on numerous occasions. Slocum trusted Tewkesbury explicitly, and the feeling was mutual. It came as no surprise to Tewkesbury that Slocum came knocking on his door to seek advice at this crucial juncture in his career.

"I need to set up a top-notch campaign team, and I want you to be my campaign manager," Slocum got right to the point. "I need to find a way to win when the odds are completely against me."

Playing the odds was Tewkesbury's forte. He lived and died by the sight of small differences that to the average man might seem insignificant but to an experienced professional, like himself, spelled the difference between winning and losing. To Tewkesbury, statistical significance had its place, but rare, statistically insignificant events were much more exciting and, in many ways, much more meaningful. As Tewkesbury was aware, there were many examples of rare events in biology, but they also occurred in politics. For example, of all the presidents of the United States since 1888, only George W. Bush became president in 2000 even though he lost the popular vote. That rare event completely changed the direction of the country. Tewkesbury understood that in politics, rare events could be game changers.

"When do you need my answer?" Tewkesbury asked.

"Like, yesterday. I need to campaign, and every day gone is a day lost."

"Okay, I will do it," Tewksbury responded, barely pausing to consider as he jumped on the political bandwagon. "We have a lot of work to do. First, I will set up a team, then I will run a poll. That should help us decide the strategy for the campaign. In the meantime, go and kiss lots of babies. I want you out there shaking hands and smiling a lot. And make sure your hair is always combed. Let the people get to know the real you."

Slocum was afraid of that. "I hope they never get to do that," he responded.

Not comfortable in the limelight, Slocum certainly did not want to air his dirty laundry in public. Politics could be unforgiving, and in all likelihood, he would not come out unscathed at the end of that long tunnel leading to the voting booth.

"And all for what? In business, I could make at least ten times the president's yearly salary, and nobody would care a stitch who I laid last night as long as I delivered results," he grumbled.

By late December of the third year of the Breckenridge presidency, after several televised debates in which he avoided having an "Oops!" moment, as Rick Perry did in his televised debate the first time he ran for president, and after a score of primaries, Slocum finally emerged as the presumptive Republican nominee for president of the United States. He was a war hero and a veteran of the war in Afghanistan who, it was claimed, was tougher than nails and more solid because of the shrapnel that was still imbedded in his body.

Chapter 6

IN THE FINAL year of the Breckenridge presidency, both presidential candidates were in full campaign mode, crisscrossing the country making speeches, shaking hands, kissing babies, and attending county fairs. Worthing and Bunting began their campaign in the heartland of America, and it radiated from there across the country. Everywhere, throngs of people greeted them warmly and enthusiastically. Crowds were filled with women dressed in their finest attire, their makeup heavily done, looking like movie stars so they could be admired by Bunting and be seen by the press and the television cameras covering the event. Men enjoyed ogling Worthing, and women appreciated Worthing for her accomplishments and intellect and Bunting for his sex appeal. Bunting had that certain bachelor charm and easy smile that women appreciated, perhaps too much so, and he reciprocated with a warm hug and an adoring glance. It appeared that Bunting was beginning to earn his keep and Democrats enjoyed what seemed to most people to be a foregone conclusion to the presidential race.

Bunting had his groupies, and the press took notice. Columns were written about alleged sightings and sexual encounters, but nothing was proven. The campaign staff had its hands full keeping an eye on Bunting and trying to curtail his extracurricular activities. Having Bunting on the ticket had its benefits, but it also had its risks. The train left the station, however, and some thought that it was too late to alter the choice for vice president. But a number of influential Democratic leaders wondered if there was still time to reconsider the slate. They reasoned that the Democratic National Convention, scheduled for early September, was not yet held, so anything was still possible. The prevailing wisdom, however, was that it would be a mere formality with the election now clearly secured by the Democrats. The country was satisfied with the president's performance, and that raised the confidence of Democrats for a return to the White House and to Congress.

Republicans, on the other hand, appeared to have little chance of being elected as one of their own was on the ticket of the opposing party. It was déjà vu. Slocum did not yet select his running mate as none of the presidential aspirants appealed to him. Most of the potential candidates either were too much to the center or to the left of center, and none were probusiness enough for his taste.

Slocum had a tough take-no-prisoners approach to his campaign. None of this namby-pamby stuff worked well for him. He needed a like-minded candidate to emerge, but so far, none appeared on his radar. He continued to campaign alone, trying to solidify his Republican base while attempting to make inroads into Democratic strongholds. It was not easy. He needed a big break but saw none on the horizon.

"Tewkesbury better come up with something soon, or we are not going to make it," he concluded. He was not accustomed to losing.

In mid-May, Slocum was still running twenty points behind Worthing in most polls, and his campaign was running out of ideas. True, candidates often got a bounce after their national conventions, but it quickly faded as they got closer to the general election. It seemed hopeless for the Republicans, and Tewkesbury was concerned.

He was watching the polls closely. For Slocum to win in November, something dramatic had to happen to sway the tide against the president. But what could that be? He had no clue.

Of course, I could initiate a sinister course of action that would result in a change in political direction, Tewkesbury thought, *but was that what should be done, especially now?* In the 1970s, they called it dirty tricks. Today, changing political direction by lies, innuendo, and negative ads was politics as usual.

President Richard Nixon was the master of political dirty tricks and was referred to as Tricky Dicky for good reason. In 1972, while running for reelection, he played his most daring dirty trick of all. An investigation of a break-in at the Democratic National Committee headquarters located in the Watergate office complex in Washington, DC, connected the burglars to a slush fund used by the Committee for the Reelection of the President. Unfortunately for Nixon, he attempted to cover up his administration's involvement in the break-in that eventually led to his resignation from office on August 9, 1974, the only resignation of a president of the United States in history. The scandal also resulted in the indictment, trial, conviction, and incarceration of forty-three people, including dozens of top administration officials.

Many years passed since Nixon was in office, and Tewkesbury knew that political dirty tricks improved substantially since then. No longer were break-ins or other illegal activities needed to sway the voters against the opposing candidate. Negative political ads and blatant lies, on television and on social media, were much more effective, much less risky and, above all, legal. Republican candidate George H. W. Bush became president after he ran the Willie Horton ad in 1989, which was instrumental in stopping the upward momentum of the Democratic candidate for president, Michael Dukakis. Similarly, in 2004, his son, George W. Bush, easily won reelection after running the Swift Boat ad, which stopped his opponent, John Kerry, completely in his tracks.

With his experience in polling and his time in combat in Afghanistan, Tewkesbury was all too familiar with the notion of "fight dirty, fight hard, and do whatever it takes to win." That was how he survived the war in the Middle East, and that was how he was going to orchestrate a win for Slocum in November. Election politics, Tewkesbury felt, was similar to military combat with the exception that carrying a gun was not a requirement. Slocum would have to fight his Democratic adversary using all available tactics, including fighting dirty, if necessary, as long as it was legal. Tewkesbury was not going to repeat

Nixon's mistakes. Nixon should have burned the tapes when he had the chance. Unlike Nixon, Tewkesbury was not going to leave any evidence of wrongdoing behind after the November election was over.

Slocum and Tewkesbury met one afternoon to discuss strategy.

"I know you said that you did not want to go negative," Tewkesbury began, "but we may have to do something that was not in our original game plan. You are way behind in the polls, and I am not sure that announcing a vice presidential pick will be sufficient to energize the voters in your favor." He paused for effect, watching Slocum's eyes for a hint of understanding. "We may have to consider something unusual to shift the tide in your direction."

Purposely cagey, Tewkesbury wanted Slocum to be able to maintain deniability should things get dicey. Slocum did not push for more information. He understood exactly what Tewkesbury was saying, although he had no idea what he had in mind. They knew each other well enough and could almost read each other's minds.

"I haven't decided yet what that something should be, but it will have to be significant. For now, I am concentrating on identifying the weakest link in Worthing's campaign that we may be able to exploit. So far, I have identified only one."

"And what is that?" Slocum's curiosity took hold.

"As best as I can tell, Bunting is the weakest link in the president's campaign. First, he is a Republican, which right away makes him a potential ally for us and a liability for her. Second, he is a highly charged male who likes women, and his behavior is often an embarrassment to the president. We can explore that and see who he cavorts with and whether we can capitalize on his sexual appetite. You may recall that in 1988, Gary Hart was considered a front-runner for the Democratic nomination for president until his philandering was revealed and he quickly faded from contention. Unlike Hart, who was married, Bunting is single, but his sexual appetite is just as strong, and like Hart, he does not mind flaunting it. There may be something there for us to explore to our benefit."

"Is there anything else?" Slocum was impatient.

"I am still researching. Like I said, I have not yet decided anything, but if things do not change soon, we may have to consider other options to improve your chances in November."

Chapter 7

THE PRESIDENT'S HUSBAND was restless. It was Memorial Day weekend, and he was looking forward to the tryst he had arranged.

It was quite awhile since he had a fling with a man, and the sexual tension he was experiencing was unbearable. Being in a pretend marriage had its difficulties ever since his wife was elected vice president and even more so when she became president and the press took greater interest in his activities. Under the pretense of visiting his aging parents in Nebraska, Worthing intended to ensconce himself in a sexual affair with a man, completely secluded and away from prying eyes. He needed that, he told himself, to relieve the constant pressures of the White House and his deteriorating marriage.

Worthing's parents were farmers for as long as he could remember. They moved to Nebraska from nearby Kansas shortly before he was born. That Nebraska was the ninth least densely populated state in the nation made settling there that much more appealing. Violent thunderstorms and tornadoes only added to its wonder and beauty. In spite of the wide variations in temperature between summer, which reached as high as 110 degrees, and winter, with record temperatures as low as forty degrees below zero, life was pleasant in rural Nebraska. His parents enjoyed toiling the land, away from the hustle and bustle of Omaha or other major cities.

When Worthing was in high school, his parents converted a barn that bordered the main house into living quarters so that he could study and live in complete quiet. The arrangement worked out well as Worthing studied hard so that he would enter the best college possible after graduation. It was also to be the place where his sexual exploration began and where he would lose his virginity.

Although he dated several pretty girls with all the sexual intentions expected of young bucks of that age, Worthing noticed that kissing girls or fondling their breasts did not excite his imagination or arouse his sexual appetite. When his friends spoke about their sexual conquests, he could not identify with their stories or with their sexual experiences. He felt alone and confused, unable to explain his lack of sexual feelings for the opposite sex. Even at a younger age, he suspected that he was gay, but it was only later that he came to accept it to be true, thanks in large part to his new living arrangements.

He began a routine of studying with a fellow male classmate. On one such occasion, when they took a break from studying, they found themselves sitting on the edge of the bed glancing longingly into each other's eyes. Without warning, his friend placed his right hand on Worthing's cheek and, with the other, lovingly stroked his hair. At first, Worthing did not know how to react, having been caught off guard. *Surely there must be something wrong with this*, he thought. But he found that he enjoyed the experience more than any of his sexual encounters with female companions. He relaxed and closed his eyes as his friend, observing the change in Worthing's demeanor, gently massaged his manhood and kissed him softly at first then deeply. Worthing found himself responding to this new sexual experience with enthusiasm. Their kissing escalated in intensity as their tongues thrust back and forth, each caressing the other like a long-lost friend—their warm, wet embrace mirrored by the movements of their undulating bodies.

For the first time, Worthing experienced an explosive orgasm the likes of which he did not experience before. Thereafter, he looked forward to their frequent rendezvous as he took full advantage of his privacy to explore sexual stirrings that awakened within him, feelings that previously he could not explain but whose meaning he now clearly understood. His parents, not knowing what went on behind the closed doors, assumed he was studying for his exams and often expressed how proud they were of his diligence.

Worthing's sexual exploration continued throughout his high school years, but upon entering college, he decided that it would be best if his sexual preference was kept a secret. Soon he would be entering the workforce where being gay might limit him professionally.

It was in his sophomore year that he considered pledging a fraternity. "Go to Rush, and attend fraternity parties," he was advised. "You will have a great time, drink beer, and make new friends, even if you do not pledge." He decided to follow this advice.

On one such occasion, Worthing attended a fraternity party that was held in a multilevel fraternity house near his dorm. By 10:00 p.m., the building overflowed with potential pledges as students gathered in small groups. They drank beer, mingled, met fraternity brothers, and circulated. Worthing did not particularly like beer, but with a can in hand, occasionally sipping his brew, he moved with the flow of the crowd and viewed photos of various fraternity events that were displayed on the walls of the upper floors. When he reached the top floor, the rooms were larger, and the displays more extensive. As he admired the photos and memorabilia, he was approached by a visiting upper-class fraternity brother who introduced himself as Bud, a nickname he acquired because he liked to drink Budweiser beer.

Bud was slightly older than Worthing, but their age difference did not seem to matter as their conversation flowed easily. They found that they had a common bond, both having been raised on a farm. Unlike Worthing who acted first, often without thinking of the possible consequences of his actions, Bud seemed to analyze everything to the point of near paralysis. Nevertheless, he was easy to talk to and was full of ideas, especially about world affairs.

"I hope to enter politics one day," Bud said between gulps of his ice-cold beer. "Only in politics can you make a real difference."

"My interests lie in business. I plan to build a successful Internet company." Worthing had his five-year plan and was ready to share his dreams with Bud.

"Oh? And what sort of a company would that be? A typical moneymaker or one that contributes to society?"

"I don't think that the two are mutually exclusive," Worthing responded. "I am thinking of forming a company that puts part-time job seekers together with employers in the service sector." He paused to let the concept sink in as he watched Bud's face for a clue of appreciation. "And best of all," Worthing emphasized, "it would contribute to society by increasing employment while, at the same time, making me money. Everybody wins. Now, what's wrong with that?"

Bud mulled the idea for a minute. "Not bad. You might have something there. When are you planning to do this?" He seemed more interested now.

"First, I have to finish college, and then I want to go to business school for my MBA, preferably at Harvard or some other Ivy League school, if possible. I suppose it is still a few years down the road, but that is what I am thinking about right now, and so far, I still think it is a good idea that is doable. How about you? What are your career plans?"

Swirling his beer, Bud noticed that the can was nearly empty. He took a final sip, burped unexpectedly, and walked over to the large tub where more beer cans were chilling in ice. He opened a new can of Budweiser, took another sip, and finally replied. "I will be starting law school next year, but after I graduate, I hope to get elected to a state political office before running for Congress. It will be a long trek, but you have to start somewhere."

"I suppose so," Worthing replied. He did not care much about politics, so he feigned interest.

They conversed a bit longer, after which Bud mentioned that he was staying in one of the guest rooms in the fraternity house and suggested that they go to his room and watch TV. After hesitating for a moment, Worthing agreed, feeling proud that an upper classman befriended him and invited him to his room.

The room was one of four guest rooms in the fraternity house that was expressly used by visiting fraternity brothers. The furnishings were sparse and included a double bed, desk, chair, a chest of drawers, and a small black-and-white TV that was strategically placed on the desk so it would be viewed while lying in bed. The bathroom and shower were in the hallway. Although the room had basic furnishings, it was sufficient for a two-to-three night stay for single students, and more importantly, the room was complimentary for visiting fraternity brothers.

Sprawling himself on the bed, Bud found a comfortable position so he could watch a popular game show. Worthing moved his chair closer to the bed and sat facing the television. Between the wooden slats on the back of the chair and the mediocre seat cushion, he was very uncomfortable. He began to squirm, sometimes sliding down as he tried to find a comfortable position.

Noticing that Worthing was uncomfortable, Bud invited Worthing to join him and watch the program from the comfort of his bed. At first, Worthing resisted, but the more he squirmed, the more he found the bed inviting. Eventually, he lay on the bed, resting his head on the large pillow and watched the game show.

They watched the program closely, occasionally laughing at the inadequacies of the contestants. At times, they shouted the answers when the contestants seemed stumped. Worthing relaxed, enjoying the soft mattress and bedding, which he found much more comfortable than the wooden chair with the hard, stiff slats on which he was sitting only moments earlier.

It was during one commercial break that Bud slowly extended his left hand toward Worthing's right hand and, finding it, held it in his own, giving it a gentle squeeze. Worthing was distracted so he did not pull his hand away. Bud, seeing this as a sign of acceptance, gently caressed Worthing's hand. When Worthing noticed what was going on, his heart began to race. He did not suspect Bud of being gay, and this turn of events left him bewildered. Bud took the initiative and moved closer to Worthing and gave him a warm hug. It was not long before they were groping at each other, rapidly removing each other's clothing. Bud kissed Worthing strongly then mounted him, letting their passion escalate. It was only later, when they lay naked in each other's arms, that they reflected on what occurred.

They saw each other often since then but never had another sexual encounter. The tryst that Worthing arranged for Memorial Day would be their first meeting since that time in the fraternity house. Worthing was understandably nervous as he paced the room, waiting for Bud to arrive.

Soon, there was a gentle knock on the door. Worthing opened the door.

"Hi, John." Bud's eyes danced with exhilaration at seeing Worthing in the doorway.

"Hello, Mr. Vice President."

Bunting smiled, leaning slightly against the doorframe.

Worthing pulled Bunting into the room and kicked the door shut behind them, kissing him profusely. They tore each other's clothing off as they fell on the bed, their passion rising. There was no time to waste. Their time together would be short, and there was much catching up to do.

Chapter 8

THE PROBLEM WITH Bunting was not that he liked men, which was not common knowledge, but that he loved women even more. Some would have labeled him bisexual, but he preferred thinking of himself as a modern heterosexual man with the added freedom of sexual exploration with his own gender whenever it suited him.

After their brief affair at the fraternity house, Bunting and Worthing parted ways as each pursued his own career. Bunting's ambition led him to politics. He was relentless in meeting his professional objectives. First, he entered local politics, and later, he was elected governor of his state, followed by a stint in Congress. He was on his way to a bright political future.

From a distance, Bunting followed Worthing's progress as he became a business entrepreneur and later married Jessica Littleton. When Worthing's wife was selected to become vice president of the United States, Bunting realized that soon the time would be right to cash in on the clandestine relationship they enjoyed when both were in their youth.

Bunting suspected that Worthing kept his sexual preference a secret and that in all likelihood, besides his wife, he was probably the only one who knew anything about it. He did not hear any mention of it in the halls of Congress or in conversations with fellow lawmakers. Nor was anything written about Worthing's sexual leanings in the tabloid press. Bunting realized that his knowledge of Worthing's sexuality and his earlier relationship with Worthing could prove to be a valuable asset as he rose within the political establishment. He aimed to capitalize on his knowledge when the time was appropriate. That opportunity arose when Jessica Worthing became president and began vetting potential candidates for vice president.

"I want to become vice president of the United States," Bunting approached Worthing one day as they breakfasted over coffee and pastry in the White House mess hall.

Eating his food quickly without letting it digest properly was not something Worthing ordinarily did. He washed down the pastry with a sip of his coffee before responding. "And how are you going to do that?"

"You are going to recommend me to the president," Bunting casually replied. Worthing looked at Bunting with a puzzled expression on his face as he took another sip of his coffee. "And why would I want to do that?" he asked and resumed eating.

"Let's just say that we go back a long way. I would hope that for old times' sake, you would want to do this for me." Bunting reached over and with his pinky, stroked Worthing's hand ever so gently. This startled Worthing, who looked around every which way and quickly withdrew his hand lest anyone notice.

"I am not insinuating anything," Bunting continued, "but I know things, and I want things to remain as they are, as I am sure you do too. Nevertheless, should I inadvertently let something slip off the tip of my tongue . . . ?" He let the thought dangle in midair, leaving Worthing to contemplate the meaning of his remarks.

"You wouldn't do that"—Worthing looked downcast—"would you?" His heart raced as he imagined what would happen if the press got a whiff of the secret he was harboring all those years. His world would be ruined, and his wife would surely lose the general election when she inevitably ran for her own term as president.

"Of course I wouldn't," Bunting replied, looking very serious, "but you never know what might be said inadvertently at a moment of weakness." He paused for effect, letting his words sink in and allowing sufficient time for Worthing to consider his request.

"Do this for me, just this once. Simply mention my name to the president. That is all. What do you have to lose? I know there are no guarantees, but your recommendation is all I ask. I will take it from there."

It did not take long for Worthing to convince the president that selecting Bunting, a Republican, to be her vice president would be good for the country and, just as important, an idea that would be looked upon as bold and innovative. It would immediately catapult her into a favorable standing during a very difficult time. After consulting with her campaign manager, she agreed.

Chapter 9

SCHOOLS WERE GETTING ready to close for the summer by mid-June, and children were looking forward to their end-of-year vacation. Ohio was shaping up to be a swing state once again. Worthing and Bunting campaigned hard there to electrify young people to vote for the Democratic ticket. The president counted on Bunting to bring large numbers of Ohio singles, especially young women, to the Democratic Party, but he was proving to be a liability to the campaign.

On their first day in Cincinnati, Bunting was photographed in a red Mustang convertible with a pretty blond-haired young woman seated next to him. Both were smiling with a can of beer in hand as they parked by the side of the road, enjoying the view of the Ohio River. A closer examination of the picture showed Bunting's right hand resting on the woman's knee, completely covered by the hemline of her skirt. The photo appeared on every major newspaper in the nation with the caption, "How high will Bunting go?" Although Bunting was single, his behavior at this crucial moment in the campaign was proving to be an embarrassment to the administration.

When Bunting learned that the campaign organized a trip to Ohio, he did not hesitate to contact Jennifer Sweet, a flight attendant for American Airlines who resided in Cincinnati. Sweet, whose routes often took her to DC, met the vice president on one of those occasions. Anticipating a campaign stop in Ohio, Bunting was eager to seek the solace and comfort of Sweet's bosom while he campaigned in the state. She, in turn, quickly changed her work schedule to accommodate the vice president.

"What is wrong with you?" Worthing admonished the vice president when they met in the Oval Office. "We are in a political campaign, not the dating game. Don't you realize that everything you do is magnified ten times over?" She was upset, and it showed.

"We were only out on an afternoon outing. That is all. Simply a couple on an afternoon date. One minute we were alone, and the next minute, I find a photo on the front pages of major newspapers and assorted tabloids."

Bunting paused to catch his breath. "And the picture does not depict at all what actually happened," he added, his voice rising, which infuriated Worthing even further.

"Spare me the details." The president was now downright angry. "I am really not interested. You can sleep with her all you want for all I care. The only thing that is important to me right now is, do you want to remain on the ticket or not?" She looked him straight in the eye with as stern a look as she could muster.

Ever the politician, Bunting rose and paced in front of the president as he considered the question. He was a Republican on a Democratic ticket for vice president of the United States. There were benefits, of course, but he was hearing lots of negative comments from Republicans who thought it was a bad idea. It did not benefit the party, and there was some question about whether or not it benefited him politically. After all, by being on the Democratic ticket, it could be interpreted by some that he was supporting the opposition for personal gain.

"For the good of the country," he said finally, "I am in it as long as you want me, but I am also a single red-blooded American man with a private life. You cannot expect me to stop being myself. I am not cheating on a wife. I am not having liaisons with prostitutes. I am simply doing what any single red-blooded American male would do, and if that is a problem for the press, then screw them." Bunting was enraged, and he quickened his pace.

For a moment, Worthing feared that Bunting was aware of her secret. But how could he know? She searched his eyes for a sign but did not see anything that suggested that he knew her predicament. She decided that there was no way he could know about her sexual preference. That eased her mind considerably but not completely. Was it possible that he knew something, and if so, what was it? She was still uneasy.

"Sit down, will you? You are giving me a neck ache just trying to follow you." Worthing was anxious to get the matter over with and quickly. "Nobody is complaining about your virility or sexual prowess, which I am sure is considerable. I am simply saying that being vice president comes with a certain level of responsibility above and beyond those of the duties of the Office. Appearance matters. Perception matters. What you do matters." She swiveled her chair to face him directly. "What you do behind closed doors is your business," she said. "What you do in public is my business. Understood?"

Bunting squirmed in his chair as his eyes locked in with those of the president. Although they had political differences, he respected Worthing for her intellect and drive. She was placed in a difficult position after the death of Breckenridge but rose to the occasion. All in all, she did a remarkable job under very trying circumstances. He supported her efforts. When they had differences, they aired and resolved them in private then showed a united front in public. Worthing chose him when she could have chosen someone from her own party. She gave him a chance to make history. He definitely owed her one.

"And one more thing, I am being pressured to remove you from the ticket and to select a Democrat for vice president. So far, I resisted. If you want to stay on the ticket, please do not make it easy for them. I may not be able to resist them much longer if you insist on continuing on the path you have taken lately. Do I make myself clear?" Worthing raised her voice for emphasis and looked sternly at Bunting, whose knees began to shake. He assumed that the "them" that Worthing was referring to were the elder statesmen of the Democratic Party. He nodded, excused himself, and left the Oval Office.

It was hard to take a verbal tongue lashing from the president, especially when she was right. Bunting reviewed what transpired and agreed that he must watch his personal life more closely, or his political life would wind up in a shambles. He saw Worthing's sudden change in composure when he explained his behavior as being typical of any American male. Her eyes seemed to take on a worried look, and her mouth opened slightly, as if ready to let out a cry. What did he say that raised a specter of concern in Worthing's eyes? He could not recall. He was too emotional at the time to pay attention, and he did not remember a word he said that would have set off such a reaction from the president. He wondered if his imagination was running away from him.

In the Oval Office, Worthing put her head back in her chair, closed her eyes, and reflected on the current state of her campaign. It was generally going well even though there were a few hiccups here and there. It was only June, and anything could still happen before the general election, and it usually did. For now, she would keep Bunting on the ticket. He provided continuity and some easing of tension between the Democrats and the Republicans. True, he had his quirks, but somehow she would have to deal with them. And when she weighed the pluses and minuses of having him remain on the ticket, the benefits definitely outweighed his negatives by a long shot. She would not have to make her final decision until the Democratic National Convention in September, and that gave her about three months to decide. Hopefully, she would be able to keep the Democratic Party leaders at bay until then.

As far as Bunting's remarks were concerned, Worthing concluded that he could not possibly have any suspicions about her sexual leanings. She kept her secret well, and her husband was the only other person who was aware of it, and he had his own secret to maintain. It would be very unlikely that he would have mentioned her secret to anybody. It would not only jeopardize her future but his future as well. True, Bunting was reckless lately, but not enough to run into real trouble. She looked into his eyes but saw nothing that indicated that he was aware of her situation.

"I am being overly cautious," Worthing decided, "and perhaps a bit paranoid. Better to forget that the conversation ever took place and move on. Sylvia Kendall is planning a White House celebration on the Fourth of July at Camp David that promises to be lots of fun and very entertaining. It should help ease any tensions that might exist in the campaign. After all, who doesn't like fireworks, good food, dancing, and the best entertainment that the country can provide? Having members of both parties congregate and mingle in the peaceful wooded surroundings of Camp David should ensure that harmony and camaraderie would prevail." Worthing looked forward to it.

Chapter 10

KIRK FIELDING WAS a grouchy old man who walked the halls of Congress for many years. Short and disheveled, often wearing the same shirt several days in a row, he looked like a tired old man on the verge of collapse. But his slovenly appearance and demeanor were deceiving. As Senate majority leader, he wielded enormous political power, casting unpopular votes that supported the president and demeaned the opposition.

Fielding was unhappy with Worthing's running mate and urged the president on several occasions to replace him as her choice for vice president. "There is still time to make a change," he often pleaded. The Democratic National Convention was three months away, and there were many qualified candidates eager to take Bunting's place. The president resisted. Nothing would budge her from her decision, and this infuriated Fielding. Bunting's actions were unpredictable, and he was an embarrassment to the ticket on more than one occasion. The latest photo taken of the vice president and his girlfriend in Ohio was more than Fielding could bear. If he could not convince Worthing to change horses in midstream, maybe he needed help. He decided to contact Dave Singleton, the president's personal lawyer, and Chuck Dearling, her campaign manager, for assistance. They both agreed to meet Fielding one morning to discuss the Bunting problem.

As Worthing's personal lawyer, Singleton was an advisor to the Worthing family for many years. Tall and with an air of elegance and smoothness that was typical of a high-powered attorney, Singleton assisted the president's father with various business transactions as long as he could remember. It was only natural that when Jessica Littleton became of age, he would also take care of her legal affairs. By the time she graduated college, Singleton was not only Jessica Littleton's personal lawyer, but she introduced him to John Worthing, and he became Worthing's personal attorney as well. His professional and personal relationship with the Worthings grew substantially after their marriage and continued to this day. Singleton felt a personal kinship to the president, having been the overseer of her family's legal affairs for nearly forty years.

Fielding and Singleton were friends ever since Worthing entered political life. Worthing was their common bond, and that was sufficient for them to overcome any political differences they might have had. Both admired the president, and both were extremely loyal to her. But while Singleton had a personal as well as professional connection to Worthing, Fielding's loyalty was tempered by his obligation to the party. As Senate majority leader, he had to do everything possible to ensure that the Democratic Party fared well in the general election. It was this overwhelming burden that prompted him to call for a meeting to discuss the president's decision on her running mate.

Dearling, on the other hand, was Worthing's campaign manager since the days when she ran for Congress. Somewhat aloof but very focused on his mission as campaign manager, Dearling was a political operative with extensive experience. He resembled an absentminded professor, often wearing different colored socks or failing to tie his shoelaces. He would wear ties with coffee stains all over them, and his white shirts showed signs of graying from the lack of laundering.

Dearling had a long history with Worthing, having been her campaign manager for many years. She consulted with him about her decision to select Bunting as her vice-presidential running mate after she assumed the presidency, and he was helpful in finalizing her decision. As campaign manager, Dearling had a major stake in the outcome of the election. Any strategy meeting about Bunting inevitably had to include Dearling as it was his job to plan a winning campaign and to get Worthing elected to her first full-term as president in her own right.

"I hate to bring it up, but I need your assistance in a delicate matter concerning the president," Fielding addressed Singleton and Dearling as he drank his caffeine-free latte. They gathered at a local Starbucks, where they hoped they would not be recognized. Although it had many competitors, Starbucks still had the best coffee in town as far as Fielding was concerned. An added benefit was that it was close to the White House.

"You know I cannot interfere in political matters," Singleton intervened quickly, hoping to be left out of the conversation. "Besides, since when does the president take my advice when it comes to politics?"

There were several problems in the campaign that Dearling was aware of, and he did not want to second-guess Fielding. "What exactly is the problem?" he enquired.

"It is regarding the vice president," Fielding began. "I don't know where else to turn. I tried speaking with the president, but she doesn't want to listen to me when it comes to Bunting."

"Oh, that." Singleton frowned and took a bite of his chocolate-flavored croissant. "Now I see what this is all about. You saw the picture."

"Has he done anything else since then that I don't know about?" Dearling sounded concerned and looked at both men for reassurance.

"I was not the only one who saw the picture, and no, he has not done anything else, at least not as far as I know." Fielding had no further details to share. "What are we supposed to do? He is an embarrassment to the ticket. I don't think Bunting is much of an asset, but he is proving to be quite a liability." Fielding was frustrated, and it showed on his face as he took another sip of his coffee.

"What does the president say?" Singleton felt uneasy by this conversation. He didn't want to get involved in political matters. Fielding was a friend, but he was asking him to interfere with Worthing on a political matter because of his personal relationship with the president. He felt uncomfortable doing that.

"She wants to give him another chance. She thinks removing Bunting from the ticket now would have a negative impact on the campaign and that it will look like she caved in or is weak and unable to handle the situation. What do you think, Chuck?" Fielding addressed Worthing's campaign manager, who was munching on a toasted sesame bagel that was oozing cream cheese from all sides.

Dearling was apprehensive. Republicans were far behind in the polls. They were looking for anything that would give them an edge. "I know the president feels that the Republicans will pounce on her and paint her as indecisive if she removes Bunting. Frankly, I agree with her. This is not the best time to remove the vice president from the ticket. Besides, although there was a small drop in the polls since the picture hit the news, we are still ahead of Slocum by a mile."

"She does have a point, doesn't she?" Singleton turned the question back on Fielding, who felt dejected.

"I suppose so," Fielding reluctantly agreed. "But something has to be done. We cannot just continue going on like this and do nothing. Who knows what Bunting will do next?"

Drinking his coffee in silence, Singleton wished that the conversation would end. He had no advice to give Fielding, and he didn't want to get involved. He was the president's lawyer, not her political advisor. Dearling was Worthing's campaign manager and was in charge of her campaign. It was his opinion that mattered most no matter what he thought.

Fielding was nervous. The presidential campaign was moving along, and soon it would be September when the Democratic National Convention would be held. The longer they waited, the less likely that Bunting would be replaced.

"Look, the White House is planning a Fourth of July celebration at Camp David," Dearling finally interrupted as Singleton listened attentively, having finished eating his second breakfast of the day. "Why don't we wait and see how Bunting behaves at the event? Hopefully, everything will go smoothly, and we can move past this as if nothing happened. But if by some chance he is involved in another embarrassing moment, then I will approach the president and see what can be done."

"Another incident certainly will add new food for thought for the president and more coal on the fire," Singleton chimed in. "I am sure she will consider any new incident in the most unfavorable light."

Fielding slowly got out of his chair. He realized that that was as far as either man was willing to go on the matter at this time. Worthing said that she would give Bunting one more chance, so maybe the Fourth of July celebration would be that final chance that would sway the conversation one way or the other. He bid Singleton and Dearling good-bye and headed back to his office having accomplished nothing.

Chapter 11

THE WHITE HOUSE Social Office, located in the East Wing of the White House, was headed by the Social Secretary, Sylvia Kendall. It was supported by the White House Graphics and Calligraphy Office. The staff planned all the White House functions in coordination with the White House chief usher and the chief of protocol of the United States.

A veteran of the special events industry, Sylvia Kendall was originally from New York City. She earned a master of science degree in public relations from the Newhouse School of Communications at Syracuse University. Honing her craft by working as an account executive in a Washington, DC, public relations firm, she eventually started her own practice as a special events coordinator for weddings and corporate events. In the course of coordinating the annual gala for the International Special Events Society, she was introduced to Jessica Worthing, who attended the event as a guest. They hit it off, after which, the then congresswoman selected Kendall to be her director of Communications and Special Events. When Worthing became vice president, Kendall assisted her with social events and acted as her press secretary to ensure that her agenda was presented favorably in the media and that she was well connected in political circles. When Worthing became president, Kendall was made White House Social Secretary.

Kendall excelled at her job mainly because of her extensive address book combined with her ability for flattery and strong work ethic. She planned White House social events that ranged from intimate teas to state dinners. Her events were always extremely well organized and well attended. Planning special events was definitely Kendall's forte. Each event was an occasion to which people looked forward to being invited.

She was almost giddy as she met with Dearling in early June to propose an idea. Dearling was busy orchestrating a winning strategy for the president to be elected the first woman president of the United States in her own right. So far, everything seemed to be going according to plan.

"What a better way to trump the hype and attention that a televised Republican National Convention will provide than to hold a party celebrating the nation's independence at the presidential retreat at Camp David a month before the convention?" Kendall said.

Camp David was a site for many high diplomatic meetings and negotiations with foreign dignitaries, but it would be the first time that the venue would be used for a White House party.

"Since it will be attended by the president, the vice president, and the presumptive Republican nominee for president, it will be a lovefest that will play well in the press and will show a united American political front to the rest of the country and the world," she added, beaming.

"Brilliant," Dearling agreed as he gave his approval. The president already exhibited her toughness by selecting Bunting, a Republican, as her running mate. Having Slocum attend such an event would be in keeping with the president's image of not being afraid to meet her opponent at any time and on any occasion. "I am sure that it should benefit the president in the long run," he said. "Considering the venue, a peaceful oasis in suburban Maryland in the midst of restful trees and log cabins, it will be so American that it will definitely work in her favor. We will need a program of activities that will not only be appropriate for the occasion but will emphasize the issues that are important to the president."

Drafting a program for a White House event is not an easy matter. No two occasions are alike, so planning one does not lend itself to a cookie-cutter approach. The challenge for Kendall was to prepare a program that would be fun and entertaining, in keeping with the spirit of Independence Day yet hit all the main themes of the Worthing administration. Kendall also wanted to showcase the capabilities and efficiency of the White House Social Office. She planned to procure the best florists, musicians, calligraphers, and photographers to ensure that everything would go smoothly and without a hitch.

The invitation arrived in Tewkesbury's inbox on the twentieth of June. As far as he could recall, Camp David was never used for a bipartisan Fourth of July celebration before. It was a great idea. Certainly the venue would be very relaxing, situated in the woods with a stream nearby and cabins dispersed all over the shaded grounds. Everybody who was anybody most probably would be invited, including many congressional leaders on both sides of the aisle. Apparently for once, détente would be practiced between the Democrats and the Republicans.

Tewkesbury wondered if the occasion would lend itself to a political gain for the Republicans. The most recent poll showed Slocum still running well behind Worthing, but he managed to make some inroads into her lead. He was now only fifteen points behind the Democrats, a five-point gain over the previous three weeks.

"Hello," Tewkesbury picked up the phone and heard Slocum's voice on the other end. "What's going on?"

"Did you receive the invitation to the Fourth of July party at Camp David?"

Slocum received the invitation and wanted to consult with his campaign manager about its relevance.

"Yeah, I received it this morning. What about you?"

"I got it this morning also. Did you know anything about this?"

"I heard rumors that a party was being planned by the White House, but I didn't know any of the details or who was to be invited. I am going to try to get a copy of the guest list." Tewkesbury hung up the phone and immediately called Kendall.

"Hi, Sylvia." He sounded nonchalant. "Thank you so much for the invitation to the Fourth of July celebration at Camp David. It sounds like you are going to have your hands full with that event. What a marvelous idea." He paused. "Who else is coming?"

It was Kendall's turn to feign surprise. She had a hunch that she would hear from Slocum's campaign manager.

"I hope you can come." She had a sing-song inflection in her voice that sounded a bit Southern, although she was raised in Manhattan. "We are also looking forward to seeing Danford Slocum. The president will be hosting leaders of both parties and various foreign dignitaries to help the country commemorate its independence. I promise you, it will be a wonderful affair."

Kendall was planning a fun-filled two-day program of activities that included a cocktail reception and dinner at the White House and a viewing of the fireworks from the Rose Garden. This would be followed by more festivities at Camp David and an overnight stay. Besides political and international leaders, the guest list included titans of the entertainment industry, educators, economists, and members of the Israeli Olympic Committee, who would be in town on a fund-raising mission to support their efforts to hold the summer Olympics in Israel later in July. "If a show of American political unity is what Dearling wants, he will definitely get it." It was to be a wonderful event and a great photo op for the president.

"Is it possible to get a copy of the guest list?" Tewkesbury was curious to see who else was invited.

"I will see what I can do, but you will see all the guests soon enough. Camp David was never a venue for a White House celebration before, so we are very excited. It will be a first. You can bring a guest, of course," she added.

There were only two more weeks before the event at Camp David, and Tewkesbury planned to make the most of the time he had left. The bipartisan celebration was gearing up to be another feather in the president's cap that would further help her win the election. Slocum and the Republican leaders could not refuse the White House invitation, but their appearance at the event would be a double-edged sword. It would be seen as supporting a celebration of the country's independence, but it would also appear to support the president. Tewkesbury was worried. He had to find a way to make the event also benefit Slocum.

Chapter 12

THE COUNTRY WAS ready for an uplifting celebration, and the Fourth of July was the perfect time to have one. It was early summer, and the weather was balmy. The American electorate was tired of the constant bombardment by political ads and was all too happy to spend its summer months travelling, barbecuing, or getting together with family and friends. Anything to keep them away from their television sets. Many came to Washington to witness the evening's festivities on the mall between the Lincoln Memorial and the Washington Monument. The event promised to be spectacular with top bands and guest artists displaying their talent for all to enjoy, followed by a fireworks display at 9:30 p.m., which was advertised to be the best of the best.

Tourists began their day with visits to Washington landmarks, such as the Vietnam Veterans Memorial, just across the street from the Lincoln Memorial, the museums of the Smithsonian Institution, the popular Air and Space Museum, and the National Gallery of Art. By late afternoon, the crowd was at over three hundred thousand people. They began by staking their claim to the grassy sections of the mall as they lined their blankets facing the Potomac River for the best view of the evening's festivities and fireworks. As an added treat, the National Symphony Orchestra was retained to play Tchaikovsky's *Overture of 1812*, beginning at the fireworks' finale.

Many people picnicked on food and soft drinks bought from local vendors since coolers and hard liquor were forbidden to be brought to the mall. Soon, the young and the young at heart began dancing to the latest music being played on their iPods. A party atmosphere was in the air as the crowd swelled in size by early evening to a projected attendance of five hundred thousand people.

At the East Gate of the White House, two hundred dignitaries in formal attire arrived by six o'clock in the evening and were lined up, ready to enter through the gate after first having their identification verified by the guard. The president and her husband and the vice president looked out from one of the side windows of the White House as guests gathered at the main doors, patiently waiting their turn to enter the building. It was a painstaking task to select the honored guests and dignitaries who would attend the celebratory event, but Kendall and her staff rose to the occasion and did a marvelous job of it. Danford Slocum, the presumptive Republican nominee for president, and his wife were invited, as was Jennifer Sweet, the vice president's guest. The Republican campaign manager, George Tewkesbury, and his guest attended, as did Chuck Dearling, the Democratic campaign manager. Other political emissaries included the Senate majority leader, Kirk Fielding, and his wife; the House Speaker; and several congressmen and senators; as well as members of the National Security Council, titans of the business world, and representatives of the entertainment industry. Rounding out the list of invitees were members of the Israeli Olympic Committee, some of whom attended wearing skullcaps, the Jewish traditional head covering, and were here to raise funds for the Olympics.

Tight security was palpable at the East Gate as photo identification cards were checked against a master list of invitees provided by Kendall's office. The White House was not going to be embarrassed this time as it was in

November 2009 when Michaele and Tareq Salahi crashed a state dinner for Indian Prime Minister Manmohan Singh. Identities were checked and double-checked, and no one was admitted to the White House who was not specifically listed on the official guest list, which was prepared by Kendall's office. Moreover, a head count by Kendall ensured that only two hundred people entered the White House.

After completing their security check, all the guests were escorted to the East Room of the White House, where soft music was being played by a six-piece string ensemble. White-gloved butlers served California wine and hot hors d'oeuvres to everyone who entered the building.

At about six thirty, after all the guests arrived, President Worthing and her husband were introduced to loud and enthusiastic applause. They made their grand entrance into the East Room, smiling and shaking hands with well-wishers who gathered around them as if they were Roman gods. Seeing Danford Slocum at the other end of the room, the Worthings slowly made their way toward him, allowing the official White House photographer to capture an instant of political unity as the two candidates for president of the United States and their spouses smiled and shook hands. It was a moment of great theater that Worthing enjoyed, but through which

Slocum cringed. The photo would instantly be viewed on the Internet by millions of people worldwide and would be on the front pages of every major newspaper by morning, thus ensuring that Worthing's lead in the polls would be maintained or maybe even increased.

As he drank his Chardonnay, Tewkesbury saw from the corner of his eye that Vice President Bunting entered the room shortly before the president and was now conversing with the United States ambassador to China. Tewkesbury was uncomfortable in his tuxedo. It was not fitted in nearly five years, and during that time, his waistline increased by an inch and a half. His pants and jacket were tight and extremely uncomfortable. In addition, he could not close the top button of his shirt, his neck size having also increased by half an inch. He clearly was agitated but tried to appear calm and collected. He sized up Bunting's guest, whom he had never met before but definitely liked to meet now.

Jennifer Sweet looked ravishing in her long powder-blue Christian Dior evening gown with a fabric strap running across her right shoulder, leaving her left shoulder completely exposed. She wore long, dangling earrings designed by David Yurman that were made of yellow gold with a small white pearl at their base. She calmly let the vice president lead her by the arm and introduce her to various dignitaries, who smiled like schoolchildren in her presence. They fought to be close to her as they chatted and munched on finger food. Her long blond hair was expertly groomed in an updo, and her makeup was beautifully and evenly applied. Her lips were luscious in color, moisture, and appearance. At the right corner of her mouth, she painted a beauty mark, like Elizabeth Taylor and Marlene Dietrich used to do when they wanted to appear even sexier than they already were.

Tewkesbury could not stop staring at Sweet as the vice president passed her from one guest to another. His mouth was agape, and Dearling warned him to be careful or else he would be charged with sexual harassment. "I never touched her ass," he joked.

There is no doubt, Tewkesbury thought, *that Jennifer Sweet lives up to her name.* She was sweeter and more optically delicious than any vanilla crème filled doughnut he had ever eaten, and by the look of his waistline, he had eaten many. Her exposed left shoulder was so inviting that he envisioned himself kissing it incessantly. All the men gazed in her direction and for good reason. They were like flies attracted to a lit candle. However, like flies, they anticipated being burned if they approached Sweet too closely.

Sweet never attended a White House social function before, and this one promised to be even more special than previous affairs. *I can get used to this*, she thought as she smiled that special smile of hers, showing pearly white teeth that were evenly matched. Her eyes twinkled in delight as she glanced around the room, taking in the elegance of her surroundings and the enormous magnitude of the celebration to which she was invited. She changed her work schedule, and her supervisors were not happy about it as she changed it quite frequently of late. However, when she considered the benefits of attending a White House social event as a guest of the vice president compared to the possibility of losing her job, it was a no-brainer. If she played her cards right, she supposed, she could be First Lady one day, assuming that Bunting proposed and that he was elected president after Worthing's terms expired. For now, she was not going to worry about any possible job repercussions and was simply going to enjoy the moment. It was exhilarating.

When Vice President Bunting introduced Sweet to the president, Worthing's expression changed very subtly. The curvature of her mouth drooped ever so slightly, and small facial lines appeared at the corner of her eyes. The president recognized Sweet from the photo that was recently published in newspapers showing the vice president and Sweet in a compromising moment in Cincinnati.

"Why did you bring her?" she whispered in Bunting's ear as they awkwardly embraced. "I thought we spoke about this before? She is pretty, but really . . ." She let the thought dangle.

"I arranged the date before we had our meeting," the vice president replied quietly so that Sweet would not overhear him, "but I promise to break it off later this evening."

Worthing looked at the vice president, making sure that he noticed her displeasure then let her husband lead her to the next person seeking her attention. There were many more guests and dignitaries who wanted to express their appreciation for her service to the country, and she had to give them all some of her time. Her fixated smile reappeared almost instantly.

Puff pastries and miniature beef wellington treats were passed by the white-gloved waiters. Bartenders circulated around the room and poured another round of sparkling wine. Guests lingered in groups of two, three, and four around small round tables that were strategically placed in the room.

Making his way toward Dearling, Fielding glanced toward Bunting and remarked, "So far, so good. No problem from the vice president, eh?"

"Not yet, but there is still plenty of time," was Dearling's reply as he tried to get at a piece of meat that was stuck between his teeth.

Both men admired Jennifer Sweet from afar and chuckled under their breath at a snide remark Fielding made about her cleavage.

Dinner was to be served at seven thirty, and at the precise hour, Kendall signaled the head waiter to begin seating everybody at round tables of ten guests per table. In the center of each table was a centerpiece of tall seasonal flowers in clear glass vases so that guests could converse across the table without having their views obstructed. The finest White House bone china and silverware were used for the occasion, and lacy cream-colored tablecloths were on every table. Waiters in tails were everywhere, ready to serve at a moment's notice, their every movement choreographed like a symphony in motion.

Scampering around the room, Kendall made sure that all was as it should be. She paid careful attention to every detail so that harmony would reign and political discussion would be minimized. Assigned seating ensured that conversations would be light and nonconfrontational. This was a festive occasion after all, and the mood was to be celebratory.

As the evening progressed, everything was as it should be with no major mishaps. Kendall even ensured that members of the Israeli Olympic Committee were served specially prepared kosher meals. The string ensemble played background music at an unobtrusive volume. The glow of the candlelight reflected shadows of floral arrangements and candelabras on the walls. It was absolutely magical.

At precisely nine fifteen in the evening, Kendall motioned for the guests to exit to the White House Rose Garden for viewing of the fireworks. *What a wonderful way to celebrate the nation's independence*, she thought. And when the fireworks began, the oohs and ahs resounding from the lips of the most powerful and nearly powerful people in the nation and the world were heard across the veranda and as far away as the Washington Monument, or so it seemed to Kendall. She stood there, mesmerized. Kendall was happy with the way things were going, not having left anything to chance.

"This way, this way," Kendall beckoned the assembled guests before the fireworks' finale began. "Please follow me, and I will escort you to the waiting buses that will take you to Camp David. There will be plenty of time to see the finale and hear the National Symphony Orchestra as you walk toward the buses. We don't want to be late, now do we?" She turned with a big smile on her face toward the huddled dignitaries and began leading them out the door. The festivities were not over yet. They would simply continue at Camp David with music and dancing and an overnight stay.

Slocum looked at Tewkesbury, who was across the room, and noticed that the expression on his face was one of concern. Things were going too well for the president, and it was troubling. Very important political and business people were at this party, and they all appeared to be having a marvelous time. At least for a few hours, any political differences that existed were left at the White House gate. Within the walls of the White House, only laughter and downright gaiety prevailed. It seemed impossible that an event such as this would be advantageous for the Republican nominee.

The long line to the waiting buses was a sight to behold. Women wearing long evening gowns scooped their trains over their left arm while holding the arm of their escorts with their right hand. Powerful men wearing tuxedos and starched white shirts, many in tails, looked like penguins returning to the sea. Most of the guests marched in pairs, sharing conversation and wondering what surprises the rest of the evening would hold.

First on the bus were the house speaker and his wife, followed by congressional leaders of both parties and their wives. These were followed by the members of the

National Security Council, the Republican presidential challenger and his wife, and some foreign dignitaries. Jennifer Sweet inched her way slowly toward the waiting buses, a hurt expression on her face. She was anxious to board as she had an argument with the vice president earlier in the evening and he broke off their relationship. She was walking alone since the vice president was to ride in the limousine along with the president and her husband. Off in the distance, the sound of Tchaikovsky's *Overture of 1812* could be heard being played by the National Symphony Orchestra.

Without warning, a loud boom of live cannons reverberated off the walls of the White House as the fireworks' finale exploded in the night sky. Apparently as an added bonus, the National Symphony Orchestra played the *Overture of 1812* with cannons. All eyes immediately turned away from the waiting buses and toward the White House as if to get a better glimpse of the sound waves that were being generated by the cannons and the explosive fireworks overhead. This caused a momentary slowing in the forward movement of the procession as everybody watched the fireworks and waited for the orchestra to finish playing before continuing to board.

"I will never forget this moment," Fielding whispered in his wife's ear. "It really makes you proud to be an American."

When the orchestra concluded its performance, many guests applauded then resumed walking toward the waiting buses. With one large step up, Tewkesbury boarded the bus and found a seat in the back. Soon, all the remaining guests were seated, waiting for the buses to begin their journey to Camp David. There was still one final task that needed to be done, however, before the buses could depart. Kendall boarded each bus and counted the number of occupants, thereby ensuring that only two hundred guests were going to Camp David, exactly the number of guests that were invited to the celebratory event. When she was satisfied that all was in order, she signaled for the buses to leave.

The White House reception, dinner, and fireworks were only the end of the beginning of the event organized by the White House Social Office. So far, Kendall was very pleased with the way things were going. Much more partying remained to be done in the secluded confines of Catoctin Mountain Park. She was looking forward to the next morning when the festivities would be over because her nerves were beginning to shatter. A long hot bath was what she needed, but it would have to wait. There was much more to be done before rest would finally come for the weary.

Chapter 13

ON THE FIFTH of July, Bob Bacardi was chairing a meeting of the Lobbying Task Force, a major initiative at the Office of the United States Attorney General. Things got way out of hand with the members of Congress after they entered the private sector, and something had to be done about it. Word came down from the attorney general herself that an overhaul of Federal Lobbying Guidelines was her top priority. That was more than three years earlier, and the process moved at a snail's pace.

Former speaker of the house, Newt Gingrich, elevated lobbying to an art form. While running in the Republican primary for president of the United States in 2012, he declared that his activities did not constitute lobbying and that he simply was providing advice as an historian. That colorful remark clearly illustrated the deficiencies inherent in current lobbying practices and was the impetus for considering reform. But politics worked predictably slowly, and it took all this time to begin thinking seriously about an overhaul, let alone implementing one.

One idea that was being considered was a five-year moratorium before the members of Congress would be permitted to lobby their former colleagues. As expected, there was much opposition to this idea, especially from renegade Republicans who comprised the Tea Party, including the suggestion that it would deprive former Congressmen of their livelihood.

Bacardi was responsible for moving the initiative forward to the point of fruition. The attorney general counted on him to deliver, but obstacles were being placed in his way at every turn, and the finish line was far from view.

As special assistant to the attorney general, Bacardi was considered a rising star. He was young, only thirty-six years old, tall, energetic, and a graduate of the Harvard Law School, a definite plus when seeking elite status based on whom you know. He was impeccably dressed, hardworking, and self-assured. In spite of his pedigree,

Bacardi tried to make judicial improvements for all Americans, not only for the upper echelon of society that made up 1 percent of America. Although he had a girlfriend, their free time together would often be short as they had difficulty coordinating their schedules, she also having an all-consuming job as a special assistant to the Senate Foreign Relations Committee. Nevertheless, when they did manage to spend time together, it was usually at local restaurants or the theater, thus sharing their love of exotic food, music, and dance.

It came as no surprise that in the middle of chairing a session of the task force, Bacardi was handed a note by one of the summer interns, summoning him to an urgent meeting with the attorney general. It was nearly two o'clock in the afternoon.

Last to arrive to the conference room, Bacardi saw that the attorney general and her deputy, as well as the assistant attorney general of the Criminal Division and his chief of staff, were already seated. The assistant attorney general of the National Security Division also was there, which gave Bacardi goose bumps at the back of his neck. Based on the people seated around the rectangular conference table, Bacardi expected a major announcement, probably related to national security.

Addressing her inner circle, the attorney general spoke calmly, trying to avoid undue alarm. She described how a body was found that morning on the grounds of Camp David, the morning after the White House held a party there to celebrate the nation's independence. Many national and international dignitaries attended the event, and she wanted to get in front of the story before it exploded in the press. Since the body was found on Federal grounds, the Department of Justice would take the lead in the investigation. No details were known about what happened except that the body was that of a woman who was not yet identified. An autopsy was scheduled to be performed, most probably within the next twenty-four hours. A criminal investigation was possible, and a national security breach was being considered.

Everyone was attentive as the attorney general spoke. The assistant attorney general of the Criminal Division looked over to his chief of staff, who was reclining in his chair beside him, and they exchanged knowing glances. The assistant attorney general of the National Security Division could not hide his anger and dismay as he flexed his facial muscles and ground his teeth. Before the event, he expressed his concern to the attorney general that holding a White House–sponsored party at Camp David was not a good idea. Now, his fears were proved to have been correct. An incident of this magnitude never happened at Camp David. It was totally unprecedented, and so far, it was unexplained.

"I want you to find Morgan Baker and get him over here," Bacardi heard the attorney general say as she looked in his direction. "I want him here immediately, and I want him here now. This is too important to leave to amateurs."

Bacardi knew of Baker in the context of other investigations. He was one of the best private investigators in the country with an inquisitive and imaginative mind and a steadfastness that was needed to solve seemingly unsolvable crimes. The son of a former private investigator in Louisiana, he proved his mettle when he interned in the department during the Bill Clinton–Monica Lewinsky affair. It was Baker who noticed the spot on Lewinski's blue dress and arranged to have it tested for DNA. He came a long way since then. Baker was a good choice for this assignment. He was knowledgeable, thorough, and although a bit ruffled, had a certain Cajun charm that helped him get information when others could not. Bacardi decided to send Baker an e-mail and to follow it up with a phone call as soon as the meeting was adjourned.

"What about the lobbying effort?" he asked the attorney general when everybody left the room. "Are we putting it on hold?"

"No, carry on as usual. It was delayed too many times and for way too long. I want to get something to the

White House as soon as possible. Besides, I do not want the press to think that we are in panic mode."

Bacardi hesitated then asked sheepishly. "Are we in panic mode, Madame Attorney General?"

She gave him a look that sent shivers up and down his spine. Bacardi lowered his eyes and left the room, not waiting for an answer. Quickly he hurried to his desk, his tail between his legs. He did not make any brownie points with the attorney general today. It was time to contact Baker.

Chapter 14

AS KRAMER'S ASSISTANT for about ten years, Trudy came to him by a circuitous route. First, she worked at Johns Hopkins University Hospital in Baltimore, Maryland, as a nurse in the cancer ward. Then, she was employed at a Washington, DC, law firm, where she reviewed medical records. It was her experience identifying potential medical malpractice cases that piqued her interest in the forensic sciences and, ultimately, led her to a job as Kramer's assistant. It was a love-hate relationship. She loved her job because it was extremely interesting, but working with Kramer, who was very demanding, was a challenge. It took her all these years to learn to manage and control her situation so that she did not have to take any guff from her boss. She often let him know in no uncertain terms that she was the one who was in charge of the office and not him. Kramer, for his part, relented, knowing that Trudy ran the office as efficiently as he could have ever expected.

"I don't know what I would do without her," he would respond when describing his trusted assistant. He was not going to find out either. Not now. Not ever. Trudy would have to give her notice or else stay with him until hell froze over, whichever came first.

In her midthirties and not yet married, although she did have a boyfriend, Trudy was a sight to behold. She was pretty in a wholesome sort of way, somewhat like Doris Day in her heyday. Her auburn hair was usually put up in a ponytail, and she wore large dark-rimmed glasses, behind which lay beautiful green eyes. Her lips, full and sensuous, encircled a mouth from which resonated a voice that had that throaty timber reminiscent of Lauren Bacall. She could make the most mundane words sound sexy. Men were attracted to her like bears to honey. She played them long enough to maintain their interest but cut them off quickly if they tried to go beyond her imaginary limits. Anyone who attempted to step over that invisible line of propriety was banished from her inner circle forever.

Her boyfriend was a doctor, and his busy schedule kept them apart more often than they would have liked. As a third-year resident at the Walter Reed Military Medical Center, his time was rarely his own. His shifts often were long and unpredictable, but the rewards of his profession were worth any inconveniences that he had to endure. He loved being a physician and improving the health of his patients, especially when the patients were military warriors who were wounded in battle defending the United States and its values. Trudy understood the effect that military medicine had on her boyfriend and accepted it gladly. They made the most of the little time they had together by sightseeing in DC and Philadelphia or by spending it in bed having great sex. She hoped that a wedding was not far behind.

Trudy heard that Kramer was married at a young age but that it did not last. He never spoke about it, and she was not inclined to bring it up. There were no family pictures on his desk. Not even a photo of a pet. There were rumors that there was a child, but she did not know for sure. As far as she could tell, Kramer was married to his job, and that was not going to change anytime soon.

It was only yesterday that Trudy heard WMAL announce that a body was found on the grounds of Camp David, and that made her uneasy. It was about four o'clock in the afternoon when she heard the announcement, but the body was discovered that morning. Apparently, the White House held a party at Camp David to celebrate the nation's independence, and it was attended by many national and international dignitaries. Apart from that, no other details were provided, either on radio or television newscasts. Nobody seemed to know anything more. "Any new developments will be announced as they become available," was all they said, but that did not happen yet.

She rotated the dial on the radio that she kept on her desk, looking for a station that broadcast news of the developing story, but she could not find one. Everything seemed normal and mundane. Next, she turned on her newly purchased Sony HD TV that was sitting on the right corner of her desk and was perpetually tuned to CNN. Talking heads were in a heated discussion about erectile dysfunction. Apparently they were more interested in the health of the male sexual organ than in the health of the nation.

Trudy recalled reading about Watergate and when the burglary was discovered, the story initially was relegated to the back pages of the newspapers before it became headline news. The slow unfolding of the Camp David story seemed to her very similar to the Watergate episode.

It was now midmorning, almost two days after the body was found, and the only new piece of information that was being reported was that the body was of a woman in her midforties. A search of the Internet revealed no further details.

Kramer had to be picked up at Reagan National Airport at two twenty-three in the afternoon. *I hope he is not late*, Trudy thought. He was booked on a nonstop American Airlines flight from New Orleans, and she hated returning from the airport in the middle of rush hour. The drive would be horrendous at that time of day. There was always a lot of traffic, especially heading north to the Maryland suburbs. A forty-five-minute drive often became an hour and a half of bumper-to-bumper grind, and she did not look forward to it at all.

"They should put up a banner over the Welcome to Maryland sign on I-95 declaring 'Full! Next exit, Virginia.'" Traffic became unbearable, and for all intents and purposes, it seemed that New York's Long Island Expressway had finally reached Washington, DC.

The phone on her desk rang with a loud shrill.

"Trudy, I am on my way." It was Kramer.

"Where are you?"

"I am at the airport." It was ten o'clock in New Orleans, and Kramer's flight was scheduled to depart at ten fifty in the morning. "The plane is delayed, but they said that we should easily make up the time. I will be in DC more or less at the scheduled hour. Check on my arrival time, and I will meet you at National when I get there."

"Sure."

"And, Trudy, . . ." He almost forgot to tell her.

"What?" Trudy waited, knowing that Kramer often had an afterthought.

"Be careful driving." Then he added, "And one more thing . . ."

"What is that?"

"Bring me a banana. I did not have a banana in days, and I am having withdrawal symptoms." He hung up the phone.

Kramer ate at least one banana for breakfast every morning, and sometimes he ate one or two more during the day. It was difficult for him to do so when he traveled, and he often became grouchy if he did not have his usual fix of potassium. Trudy made sure that she would have plenty of bananas in the office when he returned. She would also take one in the car.

Chapter 15

SETTLING DOWN FOR the two-and-a-half-hour flight to Washington, DC, Kramer thought that it was plenty of time to contemplate the little he knew about the incident at Camp David. A body of a forty-something-year-old woman was discovered beneath a large shaded oak tree on the grounds of Camp David the morning after a White House–sponsored event celebrating the nation's independence. That was all anybody was reporting, and Kramer wondered what the lack of information could mean.

Whoever designed the seating for this American Airlines flight planned it with utmost precision, he thought. *No space was left unoccupied, and every spare inch was designed for seating additional passengers at the expense of comfort.* Seating was arranged with three seats per row on each side of the plane with an aisle separating the rows. The aisle was only big enough for a miniature tea cart to pass through. Kramer had the window seat in the tenth row, just past the first-class cabin, which was fine with him. It allowed him the solitude to gaze out the window and avoid any passengers seated to his right while letting his mind wonder aimlessly. He was not interested in making small talk with anyone.

"Hot enough for you?" Kramer did not escape. Solace was not in the cards for him today. Looking to his right with annoyance, he saw a rather obese and unkempt man seated in the aisle seat who not only took up his own seat but also part of the middle seat. Luckily for him, the middle seat was vacant and, hopefully, would remain that way. Kramer estimated that the man was probably in his fifties, although he looked older because of his massive frame. He wore a light blue-colored seersucker suit, a white shirt, a polka-dot bow tie, and a crumpled hat that showed its share of wear and tear. His glasses hung close to the tip of his nose, having slid down, probably because he was sweating like a pig. Eating a gooey candy bar—the kind that had chocolate, caramel, and nuts—he sucked his fingers and smacked his lips as he licked the chocolate off his fingers.

Behind every great man is a great behind, Kramer supposed. He wondered if there was more to this man than size, but by the look of him, he assumed there was not. He was not going to find out either as he was not interested in making conversation. *Two and a half hours of this and I just may croak.*

"I nearly missed the flight. They changed the gate, and I had to run from one gate to the other. I barely made it." The man was panting and seemingly out of breath.

Kramer wished the man would shut up and leave him alone. He felt grumpy and inhospitable and did not feel like talking. He woke up much too early after the late night with Joanne Johnson. Nevertheless, his time with Johnson was well spent and made his trip to New Orleans worth the effort.

"Please fasten your seat belt." The flight attendant leaned over and put her face close to Kramer's, smiling and showing her cleavage. The scent of Chanel No. 5 permeated his space and excited him. He looked into the sparkling blue eyes dancing in front of him, lips so luscious and perfectly contoured, evenly painted with redness. She was so close that he could read her name tag, Jennifer, above her left breast, which was a sight in itself. Kramer did not recognize the flight attendant as the same woman who was seated next to the vice president in the photograph that was recently published in many newspapers.

Now there is a vision that arrived just in time to distract me from the hideousness sitting next to me, he thought, his mind contemplating all the possibilities that it presented.

He saw Jennifer's lips move and heard words come out of her beautiful cavernous mouth, but he barely paid attention. He fidgeted with the seat belt, trying to find the ends of the straps, but she beat him to it and buckled him in, her hands all over him.

"Will you be serving drinks soon?" he mumbled, trying to make conversation. "If so, may I please have some orange juice, no ice, shaken but not stirred?" When all else failed, Kramer reverted to his James Bond alter ego as he adjusted his glasses, ensuring that she saw the twinkle in his eyes. She did and smiled, licking her lips with her sensuous tongue.

He sure is a strange one, she thought.

Kramer read her mind and gave her his business card. "Call me the next time you are in DC," he whispered in her ear, her perfume arousing his senses as he tried to act like the professional person that he was. He did not want her to think of him as a nerd with no interest in the opposite sex.

She smiled a warm and inviting smile as she leaned her head so close to his that he almost nibbled on her ear. He could feel her breath in his ear as she whispered, "I will," and touched his right arm, giving it a soft squeeze. She left to continue assisting other passengers, leaving Kramer to follow her departing posterior as it vanished from view.

She would soon run through the flight safety drill, a monotonous yet necessary part of flying. Most of the time, nobody listened to the instructions about exit doors, oxygen masks, and seat belts. But there were numerous cases of unexpected turbulence when people were hurt because they did not have their seat belts properly fastened. She was not going to let that happen on her watch.

Kramer cherished women, and he aimed to please them, whether in the bedroom or elsewhere. That they never complained about his efforts only reinforced his notion that he succeeded.

The man in the aisle seat extended his hand. "Morgan Baker."

He was trapped. Exactly what Kramer did not want to happen had now happened, and he could not do anything about it. Evasion was not an option.

"Bob Kramer," he replied and extended his hand.

He shook Baker's sweaty palm and recoiled at the sight and feel of the moisture that transferred to his hand. Rubbing noses would have been so much better. He leaned over to his left, facing the window, took out a handkerchief from his breast pocket, and wiped his hand. He did not want to encourage further interaction with Baker.

Baker looked at Kramer and frowned. *What an unfriendly guy he is.* He lowered his briefcase and kicked it below the seat in front of him only to remember that he forgot to take out a manila folder that he planned to review on the plane. He reached down again to retrieve the briefcase, but he was squeezed so tightly into his seat that he could barely reach the briefcase. He felt his white shirt dampening as he exerted. Eventually, he recovered the briefcase, removed the file, and placed the briefcase back where it belonged. He lowered his tabletop, but no sooner that he did so than the flight attendant announced to put up the tabletops, to make sure the seat belts were well secured, and to turn off all electronic equipment. So far, things were not going well for Baker. It was going to be a long flight.

When they reached cruising altitude, the captain was heard on the intercom. "This is Captain Nelson," he announced. "We have reached our cruising altitude of thirty-five thousand feet. If you look out your window and look up, you will see the Lake Pontchartrain Causeway, the longest overwater highway bridge in the world." Everybody on the plane panicked. "Just kidding," the captain immediately added.

Oy vey, Kramer thought. *We have a comedian flying this plane.*

After finally lowering his tabletop again and opening the manila folder, Baker reread the e-mail he had received only yesterday from Bob Bacardi, a staff attorney in the United States Attorney General's Office. It summoned him to Washington to assist with an investigation of a body that was found at Camp David. A follow-up call described the urgency of the matter. He immediately booked a flight to DC.

Baker's father was a private investigator for Jim Garrison, who was the district attorney of Orleans Parish in New Orleans between 1962 and 1973. He helped Garrison investigate the assassination of President John F. Kennedy. To this day, there remained a controversy whether Garrison uncovered a conspiracy behind the Kennedy assassination that was blocked from successful prosecution by the Federal government.

Like his father, Baker was also a private investigator, now over ten years. He learned everything there was to know about being a private investigator from his dad, and he learned it well. And like his father, Baker was now being asked to assist in a major investigation, the findings of which would have significant national ramifications. Unlike his father and the Kennedy assassination, however, Baker was determined that there would be no controversy at the conclusion of his investigation.

Jennifer, the flight attendant, passed Kramer a couple of more times and glanced in his direction, but he was preoccupied with his thoughts. She smiled, but he did not seem to notice. *Who is that man?* she wondered, *and why am I so attracted to him?*

Later, in the privacy of her hotel room, she decided that she knew exactly why she was attracted to Kramer. He had an aura of power, confidence, intellect, and mystique that raised her curiosity and to which she was naturally attracted. That he appeared to have money and clothes that were stylish in the Italian tradition added to his attraction. Kramer was the typical type of man she dated—intelligent, confident, and powerful. She aimed to see him again the next time she was in DC, especially now that Bunting dumped her, which was an unfortunate ending to a spectacular Fourth of July celebration.

No food was served during the flight. Not even a snack or peanuts, neither of which would have been sufficient to quench Kramer's appetite anyway. Kramer was hungry, and his stomach growled. Baker, who already ate a candy bar, was busy reading a memo in his manila folder.

The plane finally entered its final descent. Both men refrained from exchanging further words since their initial greeting. Each focused on the task that lay before them, oblivious of the other. They were sure that their chance encounter would never be repeated. Little did they know how wrong they were.

Chapter 16

AMERICAN AIRLINES FLIGHT 3286 was scheduled to land at Reagan National Airport at 2:23 p.m., but because of unforeseen delays, it was rescheduled for arrival at 2:43 p.m. As was often the case, Trudy got to the airport much too early.

It was difficult to gauge Beltway traffic at that time of day, and Trudy did not want to keep Kramer waiting. She would rather wait for him than have him wait for her. There were still thirteen minutes left before his scheduled landing, and God only knew how much more time would transpire before he retrieved his luggage and exited the terminal.

The wait was to be much longer than she anticipated. She double-parked, engine running, but soon was waved off by the airport security. She began to circle the airport.

Kramer preferred to be picked up at the airport rather than taking a taxi or Super Shuttle to his office. It gave him a chance to catch up with news while Trudy drove. But Trudy's driving made him nervous, which was a topic of conversation between them. He also did not like to be the butt of her jokes, but that was a small price to pay for being picked up at the airport by a woman the likes of Trudy. Trudy's jokes were not very funny, and as a captive audience, he sat and endured them throughout the ride. The alternative was to take a taxi and be driven by a man who tried to make conversation, something Kramer despised.

Having circled the airport three times, Trudy was now at the terminal again. It was nearly three o'clock, and she hoped that Kramer exited by now. She slowed down and glanced toward the sliding doors from which the American Airlines passengers were exiting. She did not see Kramer, but she was not waved off yet either. She figured she would stay there until security did not let her wait any longer.

People came out of the terminal and were being met by relatives and friends. Some were picked up by private automobiles while others took taxis or the Blue

Van for the commute to the city and its suburbs. Very few families arrived with children. Those who did had their hands full trying to make their way through the throngs of commuters with children in tow in one hand and carrying heavy luggage with the other. Most arrivals were men in business suits, probably here on a business trip, although there were many tourists who simply came to see the sights of the nation's capital.

Washington is not only a destination for tourists, but it is also frequented by lobbyists and contractors. The city is the center of the universe or, at the least, of the free world. All Federal regulatory agencies have their headquarters here as well as the National Institutes of Health, the world's leading research institution located in nearby Bethesda, Maryland. Embassies of most countries line Embassy Row along Connecticut Avenue and many companies have their headquarters in Virginia or in the Maryland I-270 corridor. Biotechnology laboratories are in nearby Gaithersburg, a sleepy bedroom community in Maryland, about a forty-five minutes' drive from the DC line. It is not unusual to see businessmen, scientists, and lawyers arrive in DC for scientific conferences or for meetings with Federal regulators.

Trudy was getting antsy. She waited patiently, hoping that Kramer would arrive soon so that she would not have to circle the airport again. As she waited, she saw a rather large man in a light-blue seersucker suit and crumpled hat carrying a briefcase and wheeling his carryon luggage behind him. He was obviously looking for someone as he made his way against the throngs of departing passengers trying to enter the terminal. A black Cadillac with darkened windows pulled up, and as if on cue, its trunk opened, and the man put his suitcase into the trunk. He got into the backseat and closed the door behind him, and they sped off. Trudy could barely make out the license plate. It said DOJ. She wondered who the man was and concluded that he must be important if he was being picked up by a car from the United States Department of Justice.

An airport security officer approached her vehicle, and she rolled her window down. "Yes, Officer?" she glanced over at the policeman with her usual big smile across her face. "I am picking up my boss, and he will be here any minute. His flight was delayed," she added, as if that was sufficient excuse for him to let her break all the rules instituted by the airport to ensure security. She added coyly, "May I stay here for just another couple of more minutes, *please*?" as she fluttered her long eyelashes at the officer.

The officer was a sucker for a pretty face. Although his job at the airport had the potential for high-risk situations, so far it was a fairly quiet and uneventful day. *What harm can it do to let her stay here another couple of minutes, as long as I keep an eye on her?* he thought. Besides, her beauty was exactly what he needed to relieve his sore eyes. There were very few benefits to being a guard at the airport, and this was one of them. What did have to lose?

"But don't stay too long. You wouldn't want me to get in trouble, now would you?" He grinned from ear to ear with teeth so crooked that Trudy wondered whether he was able to eat at all.

"Of course not," she responded, thankful that she did not have to circle the airport again. "It will only be a couple of more minutes. I am sure of it." It was amazing what a smile could get you nowadays, Trudy decided. *A girl's gotta do what she's gotta do.*

Off in the distance, Kramer emerged. He was conversing with an attractive flight attendant and gave her a rather long hug and a kiss on the cheek before heading toward the curb. Trudy knew better than to ask Kramer what that was all about. After putting his luggage in the backseat, he sat down in the front, trying to hide his apprehension as he buckled his seat belt more tightly than usual. With Trudy driving, he better be well prepared for any eventuality.

Trudy left a banana on the front seat, and Kramer ate it quietly, absorbed in his thoughts. He tried to keep the image of Baker sweating beside him for over two hours out of his mind. It was nearly four days since he had his potassium fix. Trudy smiled and concentrated on the traffic ahead. Within minutes, they would be on the George Washington Memorial Parkway, an easy drive on the Virginia side of the Potomac River with the Washington Monument to their right and across the water. It was a beautiful, scenic road with lots of large shaded trees, which made it a very pleasant commute. There would be plenty of time to talk when they got on the highway.

Looking out the window, Kramer took in the view. He loved Washington. The city was designed in 1791 by Pierre L'Enfant, a French artist and engineer, and it withstood the test of time. It was historical and beautiful and still had that small-town feel. Complete strangers greeted him every morning. One could never get that in cities like New York, although Kramer heard that residents of the city were beginning to get better at it. Traffic was horrendous, of course, but so what? DC was well worth it. He rarely drove himself, so he did not really know what it was like to drive from the Maryland suburbs to a downtown office every day during rush hour. Nevertheless, he was not wrong. DC had an appeal that was beyond politics.

They reached I-495, known locally simply as the Beltway, where traffic changed dramatically as they joined a multitude of anxious drivers on their way to their homes in the suburbs. Thankfully, it was not for long as they converged with I-270, another congested highway, where they exited on Montrose Road, one of the early exits in Maryland, just past Democracy Boulevard and Montgomery Mall.

As soon as Kramer was beginning to think that Trudy was uncharacteristically quiet, she began telling one of her jokes.

"A little girl was watching TV when President Worthing appeared in a political ad. Her father asked, 'Do you know who that person is?' to which the little girl replied, 'Yes. She approved this message.'"

Trudy could not stop laughing as Kramer grimaced. She usually liked her jokes more than he did.

It was not long before they reached Rockville Pike, a thoroughfare that was cluttered with fast-food chains, gas stations, and strip malls. Kramer finally asked Trudy for an update on the events at Camp David.

"The only thing I know is that the White House held an overnight party at Camp David. The morning after the event, a body of a woman in her forties was found on the grounds beneath a tree. They have not identified the body yet. An autopsy will be performed soon or maybe is being performed as we speak."

It would take awhile for the medical examiner to make a final determination on the cause of death. Preliminary findings of the autopsy might be announced sooner, but Kramer knew that the results from toxicology testing could take as long as sixty to ninety days.

He saw a sign for a Chinese restaurant that he did not notice before. "China Delight?" he read the sign.

"I know a woman who used to eat there."

"Used to? Why doesn't she eat there anymore?" He wondered.

"She died."

"Food was that bad, huh?"

Trudy was not amused. "Dave Singleton called. He wants to see you tomorrow."

"Is it about Camp David?"

"Uh-huh."

As the president's personal lawyer, if Singleton called, then they must want to make sure that the president and anyone close to her was not involved. It was an election year, and the president was running for her first full term as president. They would not want anything to interfere with the election in November.

Chapter 17

WHEN KRAMER ARRIVED at his office, he was hungry. Besides the banana that Trudy brought him and which he ate in the car, he did not eat all day. It was nearly five o'clock in the afternoon, but his body clock was one hour earlier since he was still on New Orleans time.

"They don't even give you peanuts on the plane anymore," he complained. "Air travel used to be something to look forward to. Now, it's a cattle mover, and that's no bull," he grumbled.

Set back in a converted townhouse in Rockville, Maryland, Kramer's office was inconspicuous from the outside and totally messy on the inside. There were stacks of papers all over his desk and on the floor, each pile representing a different case in which his expertise was needed. There were DUI cases, medical malpractice cases, product-liability cases, wrongful-death cases. There were defense cases and plaintiff cases. Most cases were civil, but others were criminal. They ran the gamut, which made his life interesting and academically challenging. With each case, Kramer researched and learned about new drugs, new chemicals, and new diseases. He was constantly challenged academically to build a likely scientific story of a chain of events. "A scientific jigsaw puzzle," he liked to say.

More likely than not was the mantra by which Kramer measured scientific evidence. For his opinion to be credible, 51 percent or more of the scientific evidence had to support his opinion.

Luckily for Kramer, Trudy had bananas available in the office, and he immediately began peeling one. That made it two bananas today. He was watching his weight since he noticed that it was beginning to creep up from all the delicious New Orleans gumbo that he ate over the previous few days.

"Let's get a bite to eat," he suggested to Trudy.

"Where?" she asked.

"I don't know. You want hamburgers? Greek food? Indian food? You name it. Whatever you want is fine with me." He went through a catalog of food possibilities at restaurants located nearby.

"How about we have Chinese food delivered? Talking earlier about that Chinese restaurant reminded me that I did not eat Chinese food in a long time."

"Fine." That was not Kramer's first choice, but he could not refuse. He would put off his diet for another day. It was always best to start a diet on a Monday anyway.

Not much for words when it came to eating, especially when he was hungry, Kramer could not think clearly on an empty stomach. There was a lot to think about today. *Better have dinner soon if I am not to waste the rest of my day*, he thought. Kramer had to get ready for tomorrow's meeting with Singleton, and so far, he had little information on what transpired at Camp David. Trudy phoned in the order.

"One hot and sour soup, one wonton soup, an order of egg rolls, General Tso's shrimp, and beef with broccoli," she spoke into the phone, "and put extra fortune cookies with some good fortunes please." Fortune cookies no longer provided fortunes. They did not even provide proverbs, only random sayings that made absolutely no sense.

When the food arrived, Trudy placed it on the large table in the conference room while Kramer perused the newspapers for stories on the unfolding events at

Camp David. Nothing caught his attention. There were stories about the Democratic campaign of Worthing and Bunting, and that Slocum was trailing badly in the polls. The biggest story was the preparation for the upcoming summer Olympics, which was to be held in Israel in the latter part of July. This made everybody nervous, except for the Israelis, who were confident in their security apparatus, reportedly top-notch. The Israelis were sure that they could provide safety and fun during the two weeks of competitive sport. With its high-inflation rate, Israel needed an infusion of foreign capital, and this was as good a way as any to attract money to this small democratic country in the middle of the Middle East. That a suicide bomber blew up a bus in downtown Tel Aviv only two weeks earlier was of concern, of course, but it did not deter the country from hosting these sporting events. Obviously, the International Olympic Committee agreed when they selected Israel to host the summer games.

"When and where does Singleton want to meet with me?" Kramer finally asked Trudy as he slurped his soup with a plastic spoon that was bent by the hot broth.

"He thinks it best if it was someplace that is discrete. He does not want the press to get wind of the meeting, so he made reservations at Marcel's. You've been there before. It is on the corner of Twenty-Fourth Street and

Pennsylvania Avenue in DC. They promised a nice, quiet table in the back of the restaurant so you guys can talk."

Kramer contemplated what Trudy said while she enjoyed her wonton soup. It was not his usual practice to meet clients in the back rooms of restaurants, but Singleton was not a typical client. The more he thought about it, the more he decided that there must be something fishy in Denmark. The whole situation was beginning to stink.

He ate the General Tso's shrimp and the beef with broccoli in silence. When he finished, he logged on to Yahoo's home page on his Dell desktop computer, where headlines of the daily news were prominently displayed. He scanned the news items, hoping to find some titillating morsel about the body at Camp David. Surely nearly three days after it was discovered, there should be more details available about what happened than simply that it was a body of a woman. But there was none, only that the body was taken to the morgue, an autopsy was being done, but the results were not yet available. *Where is the press? Why are they not investigating? Maybe the story is being suppressed. I cannot let my imagination run wild,* he decided. *Let the story unfold naturally, and we will see where it goes.*

Kramer could not recall ever hearing of another time when a body of any gender was found on Federal grounds, let alone at Camp David, except maybe at military installations. It was simply unheard of. Camp David was the retreat of the president of the United States, and you just would not expect to find bodies lying about on the camp grounds. Sure, there were occasional murders of spouses at military bases, and there was the time at Fort Hood when a military doctor opened fire, but those incidents were different.

In England, where the royal family had a large estate, there was an incident in 2011 when a body of a forty-six-year-old woman, who apparently was killed by hammer blows to her head by her estranged husband, was found on the Crown's estate near Windsor Castle. And on New Year's Day 2012, a body of a seventeen-year-old girl was discovered by a dog walker in the forest near the Crown Estate at Sandringham. Both of these incidents were described as suspicious and involved women, and murder was suspected or proven. "But that is England. This is America. That sort of thing simply does not happen here, especially at Camp David!"

Unlike the British Crown estates, Camp David is not an open campus where the public can enter and roam at will. There are never any public tours as there are at the White House or at the Capitol. No one ever enters Camp David without being invited and going through a security check. There is absolutely no possibility for a body to be brought into the camp and placed within the compound unless there is inside help, which is beyond imagination.

"Besides, the body was found after a White House–sponsored event. She must have been alive when she entered the compound and was possibly one of the guests at the event. Whatever happened to her must have happened while she was at the camp and not elsewhere," Kramer concluded.

Many questions swirled in Kramer's head, the most obvious being, who was this woman? What happened to her? And when did it happen? He had a sick feeling in the pit of his stomach that the mystery of the woman's death would unravel very slowly, which meant that the case would have complexities and shadings that he could not even imagine. The story would probably remain in the news for a long time. He was afraid that people would not be forthcoming. If that happened, the country could be at the brink of another Watergate.

Chapter 18

THE NEXT MORNING, after his customary breakfast of Tropicana orange juice, banana, and Taster's Choice instant coffee, Kramer drove to the District, as Washington, DC is affectionately known, for his meeting with Singleton. He hated driving, but sometimes he had to do it. He arrived at Marcel's fifteen minutes early and slowly drove past the restaurant, looking for the press or other suspicious activity. Not seeing any, he circled the block looking for a parking spot.

Marcel's is one of Washington's premier French restaurants that is frequented by tourists and residents alike. Although expensive, it serves three-, five-, and seven-course tasting menus throughout the year that change with the seasons.

Kramer often ate at Marcel's, especially on special occasions such as birthdays and holidays.

Straightening his tie, he entered the restaurant and was greeted warmly by the maître d', who immediately showed him to the back of the restaurant, where, hidden from view in a side alcove, Dave Singleton was seated. He was hunched over examining some papers, his bifocals resting comfortably on his large beaked nose. When he saw Kramer approach the table over the rim of his glasses, he stood up and extended his hand.

"Thank you very much for coming on such short notice."

Kramer shook Singleton's hand but, as usual, was not interested in small talk. He sat down and got right down to business.

"What is going on at Camp David?"

Without missing a beat, Singleton responded, "That is what we would like to know, and that is why you are here." He did not mince words and was very good at playing cat and mouse. His poker face did not give away any hint of the hand he was dealt.

"As I am sure you know," Singleton continued, "on the fifth of July, they found a body of a woman on the grounds of Camp David. That occurred on the morning after the White House held an event there that was attended by two hundred national and international dignitaries. We would like for you to find out as much as you can about what happened that weekend that would have led to the woman's death and to make sure that the president or anyone close to her was not involved or implicated. The president is busy campaigning for reelection. As you can imagine, we would not like to see this become political fodder for the Republicans."

Focusing his attention, Kramer thought about this for a minute. Singleton was fussing with his napkin. "Was the president or anyone close to her involved in the woman's death?" he asked with utmost seriousness.

There was a long pause, after which Singleton replied, "I have known the president since she was sitting on her father's knee. I am very surprised that you would even suggest such a thing."

"I understand that this may be difficult for you, but I am sure you also understand that under the circumstances, I had to ask." Kramer made a mental note that Singleton did not answer his question.

"I made arrangements for you to visit Camp David on Saturday to see for yourself the grounds and the facilities where the body was found. A visit on the weekend will raise a few suspicions. I want periodic updates, especially if you get any new information that we should know."

133

Singleton gave Kramer his business card with his direct phone number and his cell phone number. "You can reach me at any time, day or night."

Singleton wanted Kramer to understand the seriousness of the situation. "Do whatever it takes to get to the bottom of this, and get it done quickly. We do not want the press to divert attention from the campaign by trying to suggest that the president, those close to her, or those in her inner circle were somehow involved. I do not want this to turn to another Watergate fiasco. It is important that the national discussion remains focused on issues that concern the country—continued growth, keeping unemployment as low as possible, and above all, peace at home and abroad."

"I may need to hire a private investigator to assist me at some point." It was Kramer's way of saying that if he was involved in this investigation, he would leave no stone unturned. He stood up, but Singleton motioned him to sit back down for a moment longer.

"There will be no need," Singleton replied. "The Justice Department already hired one. You will visit Camp David together."

Kramer was not happy. He did not want anybody else meddling in his investigation, but he acquiesced.

"Do you know who the private investigator is?" he asked peevishly.

"Yes." Singleton paused, looked down at his notes, and read the name slowly. "A fellow named Morgan Baker, from New Orleans."

Kramer's face became ashen. He could not believe what he heard. Surely Singleton was playing a trick on him. As much as he hoped that he did not hear the name correctly, he feared that it was otherwise. He searched for an appropriate Yiddish expletive and finally muttered, "Gevalt," under his breath. "That is all I need." He stood up and was out the door before Singleton could stop his quick getaway.

Chapter 19

CAMP DAVID, ALSO known as the Naval Support Facility Thurmont, is a 125 acre mountain retreat of the president of the United States. It is located about sixty miles north of Washington, DC, in a recreational area of Catoctin Mountain Park.

"Every child should go to camp, so why should the president of the United States not do so as well?" Kramer mused.

The camp was originally built as a facility for Federal government employees and their families but was converted in 1942 to a presidential retreat named Shangri-La by President Franklin D. Roosevelt. Dwight Eisenhower later renamed it in honor of his grandson,

Dwight David Eisenhower. The compound consists of several cabins hidden throughout the woods that are connected by walking paths.

Officially, Camp David is a United States Navy installation led by an officer with the rank of commander. Sailors stationed there are mostly Seabees, and officers are mainly civil engineers. All are handpicked and must attain Yankee White security clearance, the highest level of clearance in the Department of Defense, before they can serve at the retreat. Camp sailors are supported by marines of the Marine Security Company at Camp David, one of the United States Marine Corps's most elite units. The marines are responsible for guarding the camp and are selected from the infantry after completing a battery of psychological and physical tests and specialized security training at the Marine Corps Security Forces School in Chesapeake, Virginia. They too must attain a Yankee White security clearance like their navy counterparts. It is no wonder that Camp David is reported to be one of the most secure facilities in the world.

Washington was not the most comfortable place to be outdoors on a Saturday morning in July. The temperature was hot, and the humidity could be gruesome. Add the fact that on this particular Saturday, Kramer would be coming face-to-face with Morgan Baker, and it would easily be understood why his body temperature seemed to have risen more than usual. Kramer was hot under the collar and was trying his best not to let it show.

Singleton and the Justice Department had arranged for Kramer and Baker to meet at ten o'clock in the morning at the front gate to Camp David and be escorted past the entrance by military personnel. Camp David does not appear on official maps, so Kramer hired a driver to take him there. Baker was already waiting when he arrived.

"I believe we met before," Baker said as Kramer exited the vehicle. "Looks like we meet again." He greeted Kramer warmly, and they shook hands. By the time Kramer realized it, it was too late to avoid the handshake. He took the handkerchief from his pocket for the ceremonial wiping of his palm.

"Yeah, we sat in the same row yesterday on the American Airlines flight from New Orleans," Kramer reluctantly admitted.

"I thought I recognized you. What a coincidence." Baker seemed too jovial for so early in the morning.

"Yeah, what a coincidence." Kramer smirked and looked away as he wiped his hand.

"What a shame, what a shame." Baker was now referring to the body being found at Camp David earlier in the week. "Do you know what happened?"

"Only what I heard on the radio. Apparently, it is a body of a woman. Do you know anything more?" Kramer was telling the truth. He did not know anything more and was hoping that Baker did.

"No, no, I do not. They will not tell me anything except that she appeared to be in her forties and was found the morning after a White House–sponsored Fourth of July party." Then he added, "I hope we can get to the bottom of this quickly."

What an understatement, Kramer thought. *Baker must know more than he is letting on.* He planned to stay out of his way as much as possible and thought that sharing information was out of the question.

Baker wondered why Kramer was there. Bacardi told him that Kramer would be touring the facilities with him, but he did not elaborate any further. When he asked who Kramer was and his relationship to the investigation, Bacardi described him only as a forensic toxicologist. He hoped that Kramer would not interfere with his investigation, which he thought was more in line with the kind of work that a private investigator did than of a forensic toxicologist.

Although no one claimed yet that the woman was murdered, areas of Camp David nevertheless were labeled as a crime scene. Yellow police tape could be seen off in the distance cordoning off a large area that was shaded by an overgrown oak tree.

Baker felt that his job was to try to shed as much light as possible on what happened that led to the woman's death and, more importantly, how she died. He planned to do just that.

The camp commander arrived to escort Kramer and Baker past the gate. He was all smiles and in full dress uniform with the air and demeanor of a no-nonsense naval officer. Kramer pictured the commander clicking his heels and proclaiming that there was nothing of interest to see and that they should all go home. It was not to be.

"Before we begin our tour," the commander said to Kramer's disappointment, "I want to set down a few ground rules. First, as you can imagine, Camp David is a highly classified and secured facility, so please, do not remove any items whatsoever from this compound. Take nothing from any of the cabins or off the ground, not even a stick or a rock. Nothing at all may be removed from this compound. Also, you are to leave exactly the same way that you came in and through the same gate. Third, you may not take photos anywhere, not even if you do not use a flash. Absolutely no photography is permitted past these gates. That means no iPhone photos, no videos, and it does not matter what type of camera you have, you cannot take photos in this compound. Fourth, you are to follow me closely and in a single file. Do not linger behind or go anywhere except where I take you. The camp is guarded by highly trained troops of marines who shoot first and ask questions later. You are at your own peril if you wander away on your own. And lastly, only one hour has been allocated for this tour, so please keep your questions to a minimum so we can show you everything that we have planned for you to see. Now, if there are no questions, please stay close together, and we will enter the compound." He did not wait for questions as he turned and began walking toward the turnstile. Kramer and Baker followed, making sure that they did not fall far behind for fear of being shot, which they felt was a strong possibility.

The apparent rigidity of the rules upset Kramer. *I hope it is enough time to see everything I need to see*, he worried.

Baker also was concerned. Were the instructions in accordance with the rules of the camp, or were they instituted specifically to slow down his investigation? He did not know what to think, but he did not like it one bit.

They began by going through metal detectors, getting frisked by military personnel, and receiving their ID badges. As usual, Kramer wanted to be frisked by a female guard, but he had no such luck. There were plenty of female recruits in the military, but none was seen at the gate to Camp David. Nevertheless, after completing the security check, they followed the commander through the turnstile and into the compound, where everything immediately turned green. *We are no longer in Kansas, Toto*, was Kramer's first thought as he acclimated to his new surroundings.

What immediately struck Kramer and Baker was the number of security cameras that were pointed at them from every angle and from every building. They were being watched by Big Brother as they walked the grounds, their every move recorded, reviewed, and analyzed by military personnel who monitored the feed from within one of the buildings. In addition, two specially constructed perimeters encircled the compound, including a twelve-foot high brick wall with barbed-wire fencing all around. "I suppose no illegal immigrants will be going up this wall," Kramer joked, but Baker was not amused.

Battle-ready marines marched in the shadows of the wall, their rifles secured on their shoulders, ready to stop any intruder and shoot on command. Heavy security was everywhere and not unnoticed by Kramer and Baker. *If you want to be safe and secure in Maryland, this is the place to be*, they independently concluded.

They were led past the cabins where President Richard Nixon hosted foreign dignitaries and where President Jimmy Carter held meetings in 1978 with Egyptian President Anwar al-Sadat and Israeli Prime Minister Menachem Begin that resulted in the famous Camp David Accords. They saw where President H. W. Bush's daughter, Dorothy "Doro" married Bobby Koch in 1992, and where President George W. Bush liked to entertain important international dignitaries. As they walked the gravel paths, past the cabins that President Nixon built and modernized, they saw where President Gerald Ford went snowmobiling and President Ronald Reagan went horseback riding as well as the one-hole golf course, the two swimming pools, the tennis court, the two-lane bowling alley, the skeet range, and the basketball court where President Obama enjoyed shooting hoops. Although President Jimmy Carter liked to fish, he went fly-fishing at Cunningham Falls State Park because Camp David did not have a stream or a lake that was suitable for fishing.

Forty minutes elapsed before Kramer and Baker wondered whether they would ever get to see where the body was found. After all, that was the main reason they came to Camp David, not for a tourist's view of the camp, although it certainly was interesting to see where history was made.

The camp commander sensed their anxiety, but he was purposely avoiding showing them where the body was found. He was toying with them all morning per his explicit instructions. "Show them around," he was told, "but do not rush to let them see where the body was located. We do not want them to spend too much time there or to poke around and ask too many questions. In fact, do not answer any questions. Tell them to submit their questions in writing through proper channels. Tell them that everything that goes on here is classified and top-secret since this is a military installation that is frequented by the commander-in-chief and by foreign dignitaries."

Leaving the designated path and walking past well-trimmed bushes, they finally arrived near a large, tall oak tree with very large, overhanging and shading branches, around which yellow police tape was wrapped to mark the area where the body was found. It was not far from a recreation hall in which social events were held and near small residential cabins.

Kramer circled the tree and saw that a strobe light was pointing in their direction. With the tree overgrown and in need of pruning, Kramer concluded that the beams would be interfered with by the large leaved branches. Areas of darkness undoubtedly would be formed around the tree. He easily envisioned how a body left there in the darkness of the night would not be visible to anyone who passed by. The body probably would not be discovered until morning when daylight would illuminate the shaded areas. Also, since the marines marched along the perimeter of the compound, they would not be in a position to see the body at night if it was under the tree where there was little or no illumination.

"Who discovered the body?" It was Baker who asked the first question. "I would like to speak with that person."

"My instructions are to have you direct all questions in writing through proper channels. There is nothing further that I can provide you at this time," responded the camp commander.

"You mean you cannot tell me anything else about what had happened here, or you will not? I need to see a list of everybody who was at the camp on the day of the event as well as on the days surrounding the incident, including a list of all military personnel on the base. I also want to see copies of all surveillance videos. I want to talk to people," Baker's face took on a red and angry look as his rage mounted. He was not happy with the stonewalling that he was experiencing. After all, somebody died, and it still was not known what exactly happened.

"As I said before, you will have to provide your questions and requests through proper channels. Now, if we are all ready, the time is just about up, so let us hurry and get back to the gate." The camp commander turned around, expecting them to follow.

This was the first time that Kramer and Baker looked at each other with growing apprehension. Although they reported to different people, they had similar interests in this investigation. Both felt that something was amiss and was being withheld from them. That the body was found at Camp David, a secure Federal installation, made the death highly unusual and suspect. That it was found after a White House–sponsored event made it seem even more sinister. Baker was anxious to speak to people and to inspect the property, whereas Kramer wanted to read the autopsy and toxicology reports. For now, they had an uneasy feeling that all was not what it was purported to be.

Chapter 20

IT WAS LATE afternoon by the time Baker returned to his hotel room. He wanted to call Bacardi to discuss his visit of Camp David, but he did not want to disturb him on a Saturday if he could avoid it. Bacardi probably was on the golf course at one of the local country clubs. He would wait until Monday morning.

The tour of Camp David left Baker uneasy. He was representing the United States Justice Department in an investigation of a death at Camp David, but the camp commander was stonewalling. The idea that he could not get any information about the goings-on at the camp on the days surrounding the incident was baffling. It did not bode well for the investigation and gave a hint of a possible cover-up. He sat down at the desk and outlined what he learned so far, which admittedly was not much. He tried to answer the six most important questions, namely, what, where, when, who, why, and how?

"What?" The answer to that question seemed fairly straightforward. He was investigating the death of a woman who, by all accounts, was probably in her forties. However, she was not yet identified. Perhaps in time, a missing person report would be issued, which would help him identify the body. It seemed very unlikely that the body was brought into the compound, although as far-fetched as it seemed, that possibility had to be investigated and confirmed. More likely, the woman attended the White House–sponsored event and entered the compound as a guest. But for some unknown reason that was yet to be determined, she left the compound in a body bag.

"Where?" The body was found on the grounds of Camp David beneath a large oak tree and in an area that was not properly illuminated or monitored. However, she might have died elsewhere and was placed under the tree. That too would have to be investigated.

"When?" The body was found the morning after a White House–sponsored event that was attended by two hundred prominent and powerful national and international leaders and dignitaries, including the president of the United States, her husband, and the vice president. But the woman's death could have occurred twelve to twenty hours before she was found. Hopefully, the medical examiner would shed some light on the exact time of death.

"Who?" Nobody who attended the party at Camp David was beyond reproach. Certainly none of the dignitaries, whether they were national or international leaders, would be eliminated from consideration as possible suspects. In fact, everybody who was at the compound that evening, including the president, her husband, and the vice president, was a possible suspect or person of interest until further notice.

"Why?" Baker had no clue why the woman died. Hopefully in time, the medical examiner would provide an opinion on the manner and cause of the woman's death. Was her death from natural causes, a homicide, or accidental? So far, it was still a mystery.

"How?" The answer to how the woman died would be found in the autopsy and toxicology reports. The autopsy would answer whether the body had evidence of stab wounds or a gunshot wound, which would suggest a homicide. Toxicology testing would help determine whether the death was caused by a drug overdose. Baker now appreciated why Kramer, with his background in forensic toxicology, was selected to assist in the investigation. His knowledge and expertise in pharmacology and toxicology would be needed to help understand the information presented in the autopsy and toxicology reports when they became available and in rendering an opinion on the manner and cause of the woman's death.

At this time, Baker could not provide answers to the two most important questions—why did the woman die, and how did she die? With Kramer's background and experience, he thought that Kramer would be more suited to answer those questions. However, with his investigative background, Baker felt that he was better equipped to identify who the woman was and to find out how she happened to be at Camp David in the first place and what she was doing there. He had a lot of investigating work to do, and he would probably need to subpoena people if they did not cooperate and voluntarily provide information. So far, he received no cooperation from the camp commander, but he hoped that it was not a trend of things to come.

I must get a copy of the list of the people who attended the White House event, Baker thought, *and more information on the marines and sailors who were on duty that night. Nobody can be ruled out. I also need to see the surveillance videos from Camp David. How can I get any of this done when there is so little cooperation at the camp?"* He decided that he would contact Bacardi for help.

Like Baker, Kramer sat in his office, perplexed by his morning experience at Camp David. What bothered him most was that he and Baker only had a tourist's view of the compound. They did not receive any information on what transpired on the Fourth of July or given a copy of the list of military personnel who were at the camp on the day of the event. This was a suspicious death after all, yet there was resistance by the camp commander to provide any information that would help the investigation. He peeled a banana, took a bite, and reviewed what transpired. He always thought better after eating a banana.

The investigation was turning out to be more complex than either Baker or Kramer expected. Finding a body on the grounds of Camp David was unusual enough, but they did not expect to have their efforts purposely hindered by intransigence and lack of cooperation. They wondered whether fear of potential political fallout was overshadowing their investigation and led people to hide the truth and obstruct the investigation. So far, things were not going well at all, and something had to be done about it!

Chapter 21

GLEN ECHO PARK in Maryland is a beautiful oasis of trees and a running stream that houses the Spanish Ballroom, a 1933 Art Deco building that is listed on the National Register of Historic Places. The ballroom is mainly used for dances, which are held most Saturday nights but also for art shows. Aside from the Spanish Ballroom, the park houses the Bumper Car Pavilion, where formal weddings, bar or bat mitzvahs, and corporate gatherings are held and where an art gallery, a shop, and several craft buildings are. Highlighted in the center of the park is a restored antique carousel that operates in the summer and on some evenings when special events are held in the pavilion or the ballroom.

It was at the Spanish Ballroom where Kramer would spend most of his Saturday nights swing-dancing to 1920s and 1930s big-band sounds of Jimmy Dorsey, the Glenn Miller Orchestra, and other famous musicians of the time as played by visiting bands and orchestras who came from as close as Philadelphia and as far away as England.

Kramer loved to swing-dance, having watched Dick Clark's American Bandstand as a youth. He danced his way through college and nearly all his professional life. It was part of his persona that was not known to many people. He often volunteered at the swing dances, placing wristbands on people's wrists after they paid the entrance fee. Sometimes, he would volunteer as a front-door guard, a post he likened to being a bouncer, although he preferred to consider it as a chance to meet and greet people as they came for the dance and to encourage new prospects to enjoy the evening's entertainment. He became what some had labeled a regular at the dance, being there nearly every Saturday night. After informing couples who attended the dance for the first time that the Ballroom had no heat in the winter or air conditioning in the summer, he would follow up by telling the women that they would be able to tell if their date was a real man if they lasted until midnight under those conditions. They were never amused.

After the stress of the investigation and of touring Camp David, Kramer needed a break that would provide him relief from the tension from which he was suffering. What better way than by going swing-dancing at the Spanish Ballroom, where he would be able to shake his booty and hold young beauties in his arms all night long? By luck, Sarah Stevenson was scheduled to sing Gershwin tunes that night, accompanied by the famous Matthew Stevenson Orchestra, so he went.

As one of her several part-time jobs, Laurie Gillian managed the cash register the night that Kramer went to the ballroom. She had a very wry sense of humor and fancied herself a magician. She would show off her talent with flare and a laugh by magically changing a one-dollar bill to a five-dollar bill when a patron would pay twenty-one dollars for a sixteen-dollar admission charge. Of course, she always gave the correct change, but her sense of humor was the first thing people experienced when they entered the ballroom and was an indication of the kind of entertainment that was yet to come.

After volunteering at his post and attending the complimentary dance lesson, Kramer entered the main ballroom where Sarah Stevenson was already on stage singing *"You're nobody till somebody loves you. You're nobody till somebody cares."* Kramer thought it was very apropos, considering that his investigation involved a body. He asked one of the young women standing alone to dance, and after escorting her to the front of the ballroom, near the orchestra, she quietly informed him that she was a beginner. "Take it easy with me," she implored, being apprehensive to dance in the front of the dance floor.

"It is only the front," he clarified. "It looks the same as the back, only it is in the front." Kramer thought that not wanting to dance in the front of the ballroom was like not wanting to sit in the front of a classroom. It was intimidating for no obvious reason. He would often joke that he had two left feet and if his partner had two right feet, they would make a great dance team. That would put the women at ease, or else, they would excuse themselves to dance with someone else, thinking he was too strange.

On this particular night, about 350 people attended the dance. It was a pretty good attendance for a hot summer night without air conditioning. Of course, the Matthew Stevenson Orchestra always attracted dancers to Glen Echo Park. They played in the ballroom for many years and could be counted upon to appear every third Saturday of every month. Young people, as well as many older folks, would come from as far away as Richmond, Virginia, to dance to tunes played by the orchestra, and tonight was no exception. And when the dance would be over, they would thank their partners for the dance and

155

find someone else with whom to dance. By the end of the evening, when the clock struck midnight, most would have danced with all available partners as they rotated from one person to another throughout the night.

The Matthew Stevenson Orchestra had some of the best musicians around, and as a twelve-piece orchestra, it provided a full brass sound that inspired young boys and men to get up and dance. Many young people found their soul mates on a Saturday night at Glen Echo Park. These have often culminated in surprised engagements in the middle of the Spanish Ballroom. Unfortunately, Kramer noted, once married, they would never return. Apparently, many marriages were not compatible with swing-dancing.

For Kramer, dancing was a fun way to release stress, but most importantly, it was an enjoyable form of exercise. It rejuvenated him and made him able to cope with the stresses that undoubtedly would come in the ensuing weeks as the investigation unfolded.

Chapter 22

DR. CHRISTOPHER JENKINS, medical examiner in the Maryland Office of the Chief Medical Examiner, stared at the body of a woman that was covered by a white sheet and lying on the gurney in front of him. It was 10:00 a.m., and he was ready to begin the autopsy. Having scrubbed and donned his blue medical garb and mask, all that remained was to put his unusually large hands through the surgical latex gloves that lay on the cart beside the main autopsy table. He followed this ritual more often than he cared to admit.

Earlier, he examined the powder-blue evening gown with the single shoulder strap and the high-heeled Christian Dior open-toe blue pumps that the woman wore. A smile crossed his lips as he recognized the shoes, a pair similar to the ones he recently bought his wife, only hers were black. By the dress and makeup, Jenkins concluded that the woman must have recently attended a formal event. It was consistent with everything he knew about the festivities that transpired at Camp David on the evening before the body was found.

His eyeglasses began to fog from the perspiration on his forehead. Pushing them up the bridge of his nose, he blinked several times, hoping that the vapors covering the lenses would quickly evaporate.

This morning's autopsy was particularly important, for it was to be performed on a body that was found at Camp David, a Federal facility and a presidential retreat. Although he had no knowledge of the circumstances surrounding the woman's death, Jenkins was keenly aware that the results of the autopsy would be scrutinized for years to come as they were for the autopsy conducted on November 22, 1963, at the National Naval Hospital in Bethesda, Maryland, on the body of President John F. Kennedy. There was no room for error or ambiguity in the autopsy. His opinions on the manner and cause of death must be conclusive and unambiguous.

Uncovering the upper portion of the corpse, Jenkins exposed the face and chest and spoke into the microphone that was directly overhead. "The body is that of a female

Caucasian who appears to be in her midforties." He carefully examined the head from all angles, looking for any abrasions or lacerations on the face and neck but did not see any.

"There is evidence of a previous rhinoplasty." He continued, speaking slowly so that the microphone would pick up his every word. "The lips are lightly covered with a radiant reddish lipstick, over which a faint layer of lip gloss was applied. The makeup is noticeable to cover unwanted blemishes, and blue eye shadow highlights the upper eyelids." He bent down for a closer look of the head. "A dark-beauty mark is painted on the left corner of the mouth." He stopped for a moment and deeply exhaled, trying to relieve some of the tension he was experiencing.

"The hair is straight and long and coiffed in an updo. The color is blond." Jenkins could see, however, that the roots were brown, which only supported his contention that blond was the new brunette. All in all, it was a very pretty face, he thought.

"There is no sign of trauma, stab wounds, or gunshot wounds. There are no lacerations, abrasions, or any other obvious signs of foul play either to the head or to the upper torso," he continued.

Examining the chest, he noted, "There is evidence of surgical breast augmentation," which he thought was not unusual in this day and age, considering that many women believed that their bosom was too small and made them less desirable. That they would elect to have breast-augmentation surgery was unfortunate because it would not always lead to attracting more men.

When Jenkins uncovered the lower half of the torso, exposing the lower extremities and genitals, he was surprised to see that the woman, who was as beautiful as any he had ever seen, had genital-reconstruction surgery with remnants of a penis readily identifiable. *Oh my god*, he thought, *this woman is a transgender*! Jenkins was keenly aware that his every word would be recorded and reviewed. He was concerned about the possible consequences of recording the fact that the woman was a transgender, so he did not mention it out loud. Instead, he swallowed hard and continued his examination.

"The belly is soft and tender." He wondered how it was possible for a woman to attend a White House–sponsored event at Camp David, the world's most secure military installation, and be found dead the following morning. He had no idea whether having a transgender at the camp was a security breach, but finding a dead woman on the grounds of the camp definitely indicated a safety concern.

After making the midline incision and before examining the internal organs, Jenkins extracted two vials of blood with a syringe directly from the heart and two additional vials from the femoral vein in the leg. These would be sent to a laboratory for drug analysis. Results of drug analysis often differed depending on whether drugs were measured in blood obtained from the heart, which was subject to reequilibration and a process called postmortem redistribution, or from the peripheral vein, which more closely resembled the general circulation.

Removing the heart from the peritoneal cavity, Jenkins placed it on a scale. It weighed 580 grams, which was significantly more than 250–350 grams, the average weight of a human heart. Next, he carefully dissected the vessels connected to the heart and observed evidence of calcium deposits and atherosclerosis of the aorta, the main artery through which blood is pumped from the heart to the rest of the body. He also saw significant narrowing of both coronary arteries.

His examination of the liver showed evidence of fatty deposits. There was also oozing of fluid from the lungs, an indication of pulmonary congestion that often is caused by aspiration. He took samples of the liver and lung tissues and placed these in small containers for later pathological examination.

Having completed his examination of the heart, liver, and lungs, Jenkins carefully inserted his gloved right hand into the cavity caused by the midline incision and located the urinary bladder. It was nearly full, so he drained the urine into a large plastic bottle and labeled the yellowish fluid for later analysis.

Next, Jenkins removed the stomach. He cut the organ in half, and inside, found remnants of digested food as well as an undigested small, round blue pill with the letter *M* imprinted in a square box on one side and the number *30* on the other side, just above the score line. He placed the tablet in a small plastic bag for further identification.

His examination of the small intestine and kidneys was unremarkable. Also, he found no evidence of a uterus or ovaries, which supported his suspicion that the body was that of a transgender.

It was time to turn the body over. Jenkins crossed the legs and arms and observed that the body did not have any bruising on the back or on the lower extremities. However, there was one more thing he had to do before his examination was completed. Covering his gloved middle finger with a substantial amount of petroleum jelly, he inserted his finger into the rectum. As he twisted and turned his finger inside the rectum, he felt the presence of a prostate, an organ that produces semen and is only found in men. This confirmed his suspicion that the body on which he conducted an autopsy was that of a transgender.

With the autopsy completed, Jenkins took off his surgical gloves, mask, and gown and sat down to review his findings. The body on the autopsy table was of a transgender who had an enlarged heart with atherosclerosis of the aorta and substantial narrowing of both coronary vessels. Without the toxicology report and the drug analysis of the woman's blood, however, he could not determine whether the woman's death was natural or unnatural or whether her death was accidental, a homicide, a suicide, or undetermined. One thing that Jenkins was able to conclude, however, was that the autopsy raised more questions than provided answers. He needed to speak to Singleton immediately before the press got wind of the autopsy findings.

Chapter 23

"HELLO, MR. SINGLETON. This is Dr. Jenkins. I just completed the autopsy, and I think you better get over here quickly."

"Why, what is going on?" Singleton sounded nervous. He did not expect to hear from Jenkins.

"I think you better get over here," Jenkins repeated. "It is a matter of great urgency that is best not discussed over the phone."

"I will be there in about a half an hour." It sounded ominous, Singleton thought.

Jenkins hung up the phone and wondered if he did the right thing calling the president's personal lawyer. Maybe he should have called someone else? Maybe he should not have called anybody at all? He decided that the information was too important not to tell Singleton. Let Singleton decide if it had any political, legal, or security consequences before he shared the information with the authorities and the press.

It seemed more than a half an hour before Singleton arrived, but in fact, he arrived earlier than he predicted. Jenkins wasted no time.

"I completed the autopsy on the woman who died at Camp David," he began. "Although the cause of death remains to be determined pending results of the toxicology report, I think it is important that you know that the woman was a transgender."

Singleton stayed silent for what seemed like an eternity as he tried to comprehend what he heard.

"What exactly are you saying, Doctor?"

"What I am saying is that this woman was born a man. Plainly speaking, she was a transgender!" Jenkins raised his voice with excitement.

"How do you know?" As soon as he said it, Singleton felt foolish for asking such a question, for who would better know than the doctor who performed the autopsy?

"She had evidence of genital reconstruction surgery, and equally important, she had a prostate. That is how!" Jenkins thought that Singleton was a bit slow to grasp the situation. He was nearly shouting. "I thought you would like to know that before I spoke to the authorities and the press."

"Yes, it was very good of you to tell me." Singleton said.

"I do not know if having a transgender at Camp David is a security breach or not. That is something that I am sure you can find out," Jenkins told Singleton, "but how she wound up dead on my autopsy table, that is a question that is beyond my comprehension."

"And one more thing," Jenkins waited for Singleton to focus his attention again. "I found an undigested small blue pill in her stomach that I am having analyzed."

"Do you know what it is?" Singleton was having trouble processing all this new information quickly.

"No, but the lab should help identify the pill and its concentration."

Singleton was not happy with the way things were developing. Here was a woman who died at Camp David, but she was not a woman, or at least, she was not born a woman. In addition, an undigested pill was found in her stomach that was not yet identified. *What is going on here?* he thought, *and what does it all mean?*

"Of course, you must meet with the authorities and tell them everything you know," Singleton advised Jenkins, "but for now, I suggest that you tell them, and correct me if I am wrong, that the results of the autopsy are inconclusive pending results of the toxicology report. This should buy us sixty to ninety days to figure out what is going on. I suggest not telling them that the body is that of a transgender or that you found a pill in her stomach. After all, we do not know the significance of any of that yet."

Jenkins was uncomfortable with this approach but did agree that at the moment, the autopsy findings were inconclusive. "I guess the only thing the press really wants to know now is the cause of death, and for that, we still do not have an answer. I suppose I can at least tell them that there were no gunshot or stab wounds. That should appease them somewhat and buy us some time."

Chapter 24

ON ANY GIVEN day, Kramer's office would look like it was hit by a wild tornado. The fax machine would be spewing spam faxes at a rapid rate, and the copier would seem to always be making multiple copies of deposition transcripts or other legal documents. Together, these machines and other incidental noises would form a cacophony of office sounds, above which one could rarely be heard, let alone think. Yet under these very unnerving and trying circumstances, Kramer would try to comprehend and analyze information in support of a case on which he was working at the time. On this particular day and under these very same trying conditions, Kramer was reviewing all he knew about what transpired at Camp David when his phone rang. It was Baker.

"Do you have a television in your office? If so, put it on. It's Dr. Jenkins. He is presenting the results of the autopsy."

Trudy turned the television on, and Kramer strained to hear Jenkins describe his examination of the autopsy above the office noise. Trudy raised the volume so he could better hear the press conference. Kramer recognized Bacardi and the Maryland chief of police standing behind Jenkins as he described his findings. Jenkins noted the absence of any bullet or knife wounds and the lack of definitive anatomical evidence on the cause of death. He mentioned how blood samples were collected for further toxicological analysis and that a conclusion on the manner and cause of death would have to wait pending results of the toxicology report.

As soon as the press conference was over, Kramer's phone rang again. It was Singleton.

"I need to see you right away," Singleton spoke softly into the phone. "It is important."

"I will be right there," Kramer replied.

When he arrived at Singleton's office, Kramer was startled to see that Baker was also there. The last time Kramer saw Baker was when they toured Camp David together. That Baker, who reported to the Justice

Department, was sitting in Singleton's office was worrisome and suggested that there was a significant development in the case that had to be managed correctly.

"I invited Baker," Singleton began, "because it is imperative that we coordinate our efforts with the Justice Department to ensure the absence of leaks and undue alarm."

Kramer was mystified but said nothing.

"Both of you heard Dr. Jenkins's press conference today," Singleton continued. "What you did not hear Jenkins say, however, is that the woman on whom he performed the autopsy was, in fact, born a man. To make it clearer, the body was that of a transgender."

Kramer's jaw dropped, and he could see that Baker's face turned pale. Both investigators were focused on Singleton's every word as they tried to analyze what they were hearing both for its meaning and nuance.

"In addition," Singleton continued, "Dr. Jenkins found a small pill in the woman's stomach, which he is having analyzed." He spoke in a monotone, trying his utmost not to fill his words with emotion.

"There is obviously more to this than meets the eye. I spoke with the Justice Department, and they are in agreement." Singleton emphasized his words so there would be no confusion or misunderstanding. "Considering the new developments, we all feel that you should now work together, combining your experience and perspective to investigating what happened at Camp David that resulted in this woman's death." He waited, but neither Kramer nor Baker asked any questions, so he continued.

"This is a very delicate matter, both from a legal and a political perspective. Who knows where the investigation will lead? It is vitally important that there be no leaks. While you will work together as a team, you, Kramer, will continue to report to me as before, and Baker will continue to report to the Justice Department. However, we do not expect any discrepancies between both of your reports. Is that clear?" Both Kramer and Baker nodded.

The idea of working side by side with Baker was not appealing to Kramer. However, with Baker's knowledge of investigative sleuthing and his own background and experience in pharmacology and toxicology, it seemed logical that working together would expedite the investigation and would be much more effective and productive than working separately.

As always, it was Baker who spoke first. "Why don't we meet and begin to strategize?" he said after Singleton left the room.

"Sounds like a plan." Kramer replied. "Let's meet in my office in an hour. The sooner we get started, the better." There was no point of arguing or resisting. "If you cannot fight them, join them" was his motto.

Chapter 25

IT WAS SHORTLY after graduating from Christopher Columbus High School that George William Jorgensen Jr. was drafted into the army, where he served as a clerk during World War II. In his book, published in 1967, Jorgensen described how when he was growing up, he had feelings that he was a woman trapped in a man's body. After being honorably discharged, he decided to act on his sexual leanings.

At the ripe young age of twenty-four, he began receiving hormone injections. By 1952, he finalized his sexual conversion by undergoing sexual reconstruction surgery in Denmark. Jorgensen returned to America in 1955 and announced to the world that he was now

Christine Jorgensen, the first transgender in the United States to publicly announce her new sexual identity.

Since 1955, transgenders had largely been shunned, with acceptance more easily achieved among young people. For example, on April 18, 2015, a transgender was crowned prom queen at Salinas High School in California, and about a week later, another transgender was named prom queen at Salt Lake School for the Performing Arts in Utah. However, although in 1977, the New York Supreme Court ruled that Renee Richards, an ophthalmologist and professional tennis player could play tennis in the US Open, it was not until 2015 that Bruce Jenner, the 1976 Olympic gold medalist in the decathlon, who was married three times with six children of his own, shocked the nation by proclaiming on national television that he always thought of himself as a girl and was undergoing treatment to become a transgender. His conversion was completed with his appearance as Caitlyn Jenner in the June edition of *Vanity Fair* magazine.

Society had a long way to go before transgenders would be accepted into the mainstream. However, in August 2015, Raffi Freedman-Gurspan, an openly transgender staff member of the White House, was hired as an outreach and recruitment director for presidential personnel. That was as close as a transgender had ever been to being at the White House without obtaining an entrance ticket. It was a step in the right direction.

Kramer suspected that few people would accept the idea of finding a body of a transgender on the grounds of Camp David, no matter how liberal-minded they were. This was something that was beyond the comprehension of most Americans and would open up a Pandora's box, full of allegations and suppositions.

"Let's review what we know so far," Baker began. "There was an overnight party at Camp David on July fourth that was sponsored by the White House and was attended by two hundred dignitaries, including the president and vice president of the United States. The day after the event, an unidentified body was found at the camp beneath a tree, and an autopsy concluded that it was of a transgender. Also, a small, undigested blue pill was discovered in the woman's stomach. Is there anything else?" He turned to Kramer, who was sitting across from him with his legs crossed.

"Nothing that I can think of," he replied. "We need to gather more facts, an activity that I believe is your specialty." He turned to Baker for acknowledgment.

"I think we can both agree," Baker picked up where Kramer left off, "that my strength is investigative while yours is forensic toxicology and cause of death. I think we should divide up the tasks accordingly so that we can be more efficient and maximize our strengths while minimizing our weaknesses."

"What do you have in mind?" Kramer asked.

"I suggest that you concentrate on identifying the pill and see if you can find out what caused the woman's death. Start by meeting with Jenkins and see if he can shed more light on the situation. Lean on him if you must."

"And what is your job in this case?" It was Kramer who now prodded Baker to lend his talents to the investigation.

"I will try to find out who the woman was, how she got to be at Camp David in the first place, and what she was doing there that may have led to her death."

"And equally important," Kramer chimed in, "was anybody else involved in her death."

"Exactly. Needless to say, we may not like what we find."

"No, I suppose not," Kramer echoed. *This may not turn out well*, he thought. *Not well at all.*

"Why don't we meet again in a few days and review what we uncovered," Baker suggested. "We do not have much time to waste. The press will have its fangs on this story like a lion on a kill. They will not let it go until the story breaks. We have to expedite our investigation so as to keep this off the front page as long as we can."

No doubt about it, Kramer thought. *We have to move faster on this, but so far, we have very few leads on which to proceed.* "Did anybody file a missing-person report yet?"

"I did not see any, but I will check again. Maybe one has been filed by now. I have a couple of other things to investigate, so I will let you know if I find out anything the next time we meet."

Chapter 26

"WHAT DO YOU think, Dr. Jenkins?" Kramer asked. "What do you think happened?"

Kramer was at the morgue to discuss the autopsy findings with Jenkins. It was important that he obtained an initial gut reaction from the medical examiner that would provide him clues for further investigation. He also wanted to see the body, which so far, he only heard about.

Jenkins was reluctant to immerse himself in the investigation. He was the medical examiner, and his responsibility was medical, not investigative. He did not have all the facts, nor did he want to give the impression that he made up his mind on the manner and cause of death. Far from it. He needed more information, including the toxicology report, and that would take more time, something that Kramer apparently did not have.

"Look, Dr. Jenkins." Kramer saw Jenkins hesitating. "I know you have a reputation to uphold and that you are queasy about getting involved. But the truth is, you are involved, and this is really a very big deal." Kramer emphasized each word to get Jenkins's attention.

"This is not about my reputation." Jenkins was infuriated that Kramer would think that he was more concerned about his reputation than his medical opinion. "For my medical opinion to matter and to make sense and for me to complete a death certificate, I simply have to get more information. I need the toxicology report. I may even need to look at previous medical records. I do not take my responsibility lightly, Dr. Kramer, when I conclude on the manner and cause of death. I would appreciate it if you do not pressure me to provide an opinion when I am not ready to do so."

Kramer could see that Jenkins could not be pushed, but he needed to get some sort of a meaningful lead from him to pursue because time was not on their side.

"I know how you feel," Kramer began, looking at Jenkins and sounding conciliatory, "but we are not talking about a run-of-the-mill death here, one that you come across every day of the week. We are talking about a death that occurred on Federal property under very suspicious circumstances. We are talking about a death that may have political overtones at a time when the president is running for reelection. We are also talking about a death, Dr. Jenkins, that may have been caused by one or more of two hundred high-ranking dignitaries who attended the event at Camp David, including, may I remind you, the president and vice president of the United States."

With his voice beginning to rise, Kramer's demeanor changed. "It is important, Doctor, that we resolve this mystery sooner rather than later. To do that, we need your help. So let me ask you once again, and this time, please think carefully before you respond. What is your gut reaction of what occurred?"

Jenkins was not happy being placed on the spot or talked to the way Kramer spoke to him. He was a doctor, not some intern. Nevertheless, he understood the importance of his opinion and wanted to at least appear helpful.

"Look," he began, "we have what appears to be a very attractive woman who would have easily blended in with the invited guests at the festivities. As you can see from her clothing over there"—he pointed to the long powder-blue gown that was draped over the chair by the corner desk—"she was dressed to the hilt and was ready to party." As usual, he was methodical in his description and unflustered. Kramer looked over to the corner where the dress was and agreed that it was a gown to be worn to a formal evening affair.

"I cannot tell you how she got to be at Camp David," he continued, "that is the job of your investigative team. But I can tell you that she apparently had a very good time." This piqued Kramer's curiosity.

"And how do you know that?" he asked with a slight upward inflection in his voice.

"Look at her dress." Jenkins picked up the dress and showed it to Kramer. "See here," he said, allowing Kramer to examine the dress closely. "Look, below the neckline, on the right side. There are faint but clearly noticeable red-wine stains. There, you see it?" He pointed to the specific spots on the dress.

Kramer looked at the red spots, bringing the dress closer to his eyes, nearly touching the dress with his nose. The spots were on the right side of the chest, almost below the right shoulder. *I do not think these spots are wine spots at all*, Kramer thought. *I think they are bloodstains.*

"Thank you for pointing them out, Doctor," Kramer said. "Why don't we have the lab analyze these spots so we can be sure exactly what they are?"

"Sure, I can do that." Jenkins picked up the dress and placed it into a large plastic bag for safekeeping.

"Did she have any needle marks on her arm?" Kramer asked nonchalantly.

"No, I did not see any," Jenkins replied. "But I did find an undigested blue pill in her stomach," he added, "which I am having analyzed."

"Any idea what it is? Did it have any markings?" Kramer wanted something to go on. Anything.

"It was a small round blue pill, maybe generic. It had the letter *M* in a square box on one side and the number *30* on the other side, just above a score line. I do not know what it all means. It can be anything."

"Well, be sure to let me know as soon as you find out. Any idea when you will have the toxicology report?" Kramer was anxious to see the report because it would help him determine the cause of death.

"It usually takes six to eight weeks, but I will contact the lab and urge them to see if they can give it high priority and hurry the testing along." Jenkins was more accommodating now. "I understand the urgency of the matter," he added before Kramer could interrupt him. "I hope their forensic toxicologist will understand it too."

"Yes, please make sure he does. Is there anything else you can tell me, Doc?" Kramer wanted to milk Jenkins as much as possible to avoid having to interview him again. At their next meeting, Baker would want to know what he found out, and he did not want to disappoint him, if at all possible.

"It may be nothing," Jenkins began, "but . . .," he hesitated.

"What?" Kramer was impatient.

"Well," Jenkins continued, "she was missing an earring. I do not know the significance of that. It could have happened anywhere. But I thought you should know," he added.

"Which earring was it? The left or the right?"

"Hmm, let me see." Jenkins frowned, wondering why it was important. "The right one, I think."

"You think, or you know? Think, Dr. Jenkins. It may be important."

Jenkins thought about it some more. "The right one. I am certain of it," he added quickly.

"Can I see the earring that you have, the one that she was wearing on her left ear?" It was Kramer's turn.

Jenkins left the room, and when he returned, he was holding a large cardboard box tightly in both hands, lest it fall and spill its contents all over the floor. The box contained all the personal effects of the dead woman. He placed the box on the desk, reached in with both hands, and began to remove one item at a time until eventually he found the remaining earring.

Taking a tweezer from his breast pocket, Kramer carefully held the earring and examined it. It was a long dangling earring made of yellow gold with a small diamond at its base. It had a stem, which Kramer knew meant that the woman had pierced ears. This would have made it difficult to lose the earring unless it was yanked off the earlobe, whether accidentally or on purpose. The red spots on the right side of the dress, just below the right ear, suggested to Kramer that the earring was violently removed from the earlobe, causing small drops of blood to fall onto the dress. Still holding the earring with his tweezers, he placed it in a small plastic bag for safekeeping, sealing the bag gently. "Here," he gave the bag to Jenkins. "You can put it back in the box."

The remaining items were scattered on the table, and Kramer began examining them closely. There was a small handbag, which he emptied. In it, he found a lipstick and other beauty products. *A woman without her lipstick*, Kramer thought, *is like coffee without milk. Both look inviting, but they do not taste the same.* There were also tissues, a pen, and a small writing pad, presumably for taking notes, and a twenty-dollar bill, probably for emergency carfare. What was most interesting to Kramer, however, were the items that were missing. He did not find an invitation to the event at Camp David, which most women often brought with them, just in case.

183

Also, there was no identification card of any kind, not a driver's license, not a credit card, not a government or military identification of any sort. This was strange and unexpected since everybody who attended the event had their identity checked at the East Gate before entering the White House. Kramer did not know what to make of it because this indicated that some sort of security breach had occurred. Moreover, without an identification card of some sort, it made it difficult, but not impossible, to identify the body. He hoped Baker would be able to have better luck in that regard.

"I need to see the body now," Kramer turned to Jenkins and proclaimed his intention. Jenkins motioned that Kramer should follow him as he turned and walked toward the refrigerated room, where bodies were placed in cold storage.

Kramer was in morgues before and was accustomed to seeing bodies lying on slabs or in drawers. Sometimes they were gruesome, as when they were shot in the head or hacked to death. At other times they looked peaceful, as if the person was sleeping. He never knew what to expect when the sheet was raised and the head was exposed. It was always a sobering experience, however.

"Are you ready?" It was Jenkins who, glancing at Kramer, wanted to make sure that he was not squeamish and was prepared to see the body. Kramer nodded, and Jenkins lowered the sheet, uncovering the head.

Kramer looked at the woman's head, trying to get an overview impression before concentrating on any part in particular. On first look, he thought that it was a beautiful head. Its eyes were closed, and the facial expression was peaceful. There was no grimacing at the mouth. No noticeable wrinkles around the eyes. It was as if the woman was sleeping, perhaps even dreaming. Serenity was what Kramer saw in that face.

Examining the head a bit closer, he noticed that the woman had pierced ears and that her right earlobe was bruised. Her makeup was expertly applied with a beauty mark painted in the left corner of her mouth. Her long blond hair was well groomed. All in all, Kramer thought that she was a very pretty woman.

"I know you mentioned to Mr. Singleton that the body was of a transgender," Kramer began as he looked at Jenkins. "Can you explain to me how you arrived at that conclusion? And please, Doctor, do not hesitate to show me anything I need to see." Kramer hoped that Jenkins got the message he was trying to convey.

Concerned about privacy issues, Jenkins thought about this for a moment. He could speak in generalities, but he knew that Kramer would not be satisfied. He would want specifics, and Jenkins was afraid of that. He would have to lift the sheet and expose the genitals, and he was not sure whether privacy laws were applicable in this instance. Kramer saw Jenkins hesitating, and he tried to reassure him.

"Let me remind you, Dr. Jenkins, that this is a Federal investigation of a possible homicide with major political and international implications. I was asked by the White House and the Justice Department to assist in the investigation. The body on this gurney is evidence of a possible crime. As part of the investigation, it is imperative that I see the body in its entirety and collect as much evidence as I deem necessary to solve the mystery of this woman's death." Kramer let that sink in for a while before continuing. "So, Dr. Jenkins, I suggest that you lift the sheet, let me see the body, and explain to me how you arrived at the conclusion that it is the body of a transgender." Kramer was getting annoyed, and it was beginning to show.

I suppose I better do what he says, Jenkins thought. *There obviously is no point arguing. He is very persistent and probably knows what he is doing or, at the least, what is legal in this situation.* He uncovered the lower half of the body, exposing the genitals and lower torso. Kramer stared long and hard without speaking. There was a deafening silence in the room that seemed eternal.

"As you can see, the woman had genital reconstruction surgery, and there appears to still remain some remnants of a penis," Jenkins pointed at the appropriate parts on the body. "In addition, a physical examination revealed that the woman had a prostate, an organ that produces semen and is only found in men. Also, if you look closely at the breasts"—Jenkins lifted the sheet uncovering the upper half—"you will see evidence of breast augmentation." Jenkins showed Kramer the stitch marks that were faintly visible below the breasts. "And lastly, she has no uterus or ovaries, although that in itself is not sufficient proof of being a transgender because some women have this surgery for medical reasons. However, taking all of this information in its entirety, I concluded that the woman was a transgender, who, unfortunately, met her demise at Camp David." Jenkins covered the body again, turned around, and looked Kramer straight in the eye.

"Now, Dr. Kramer, I told you everything I know. There is nothing further that I can tell you or show you. But how she met her demise, Dr. Kramer, or why, that is your job, isn't it?" And with that, Jenkins turned around and walked out of the room, leaving Kramer to ponder that thought by himself.

Chapter 27

"THEY ARE STONEWALLING."

Flushed with anger and perspiration, Baker was shouting at Bacardi. "The commander at Camp David gave us a tourist's view of the place with minimal time where the body was found. And when I asked him for a list of people, including marines and sailors who were at the camp on the night of the event, he refused and said that I should make my request through channels." Baker was beside himself.

"I tell you," he continued, "they gave us the runaround, and for some reason, they are stonewalling. This is unconscionable. It borders on obstruction of justice. How am I supposed to investigate this woman's death when I cannot get any cooperation?"

Bacardi let Baker vent as long as he wanted so that he would get it out of his system, but all the while, his mind was racing, trying to make sense of what he was hearing. He knew that this was a very delicate situation with political and international overtones. But still, somebody died, and it was important to find out what happened and to let the chips fall where they might. He expected cooperation at Camp David, not stonewalling.

"Tell me exactly what you found out so far and what you need me to do to help you with the investigation." As a special assistant to the United States attorney general, Bacardi had the power to move things along and get things done. He was not afraid to go the extra mile if necessary.

Baker told Bacardi about his and Kramer's tour of Camp David and how they were allowed very little time to see where the body was found. He discussed the fact that the dead woman was not yet identified.

"I need a list of all the people who attended the event," Baker began, "and I especially need to know who was at the camp that night, including staff and military personnel," to which Bacardi replied, "I will see what I can do."

"I probably will need to go back to Camp David and look at the facilities and where everybody stayed that night."

"I will do my best. We may need to get a search warrant this time, but that can be arranged. I am sure of it."

"I also need any videos that may be out there," Baker continued. "I need videos from the beginning of the event until the end."

"Do you mean also at the White House?" Bacardi asked in surprise.

"Yes." Baker was adamant. "I want videos from buildings, from lampposts, from cell phones. I want videos from the moment the guests arrived at the East Gate of the White House, as they entered the building, as well as any videos during the cocktail hour and dinner. Also, I want videos when they were watching the fireworks, when they were lined up to get on the buses, and when they finally drove off to Camp David. I also want videos taken at Camp David. I want everything there is. Everything!" Baker was fuming.

"I will get right on it." Bacardi wrote down in his pad, "Get videos from everywhere."

"Tomorrow is not soon enough," Baker told Bacardi. "Time is running out. I will also need to interview a number of people who were at the event, including the president and vice president, if necessary, and especially those involved in planning or executing the event, starting with Sylvia Kendall. I understand that she was the main organizer."

"It should not be a problem to interview Kendall. I can arrange it if you want me to. As for interviewing the president and vice president, I can arrange that also, if needed, but I will urge you to wait until it is absolutely necessary." Bacardi did not want to impose on the president and vice president's schedules until it was unavoidable.

"What is Kramer doing?" Bacardi knew that Baker and Kramer were working together but that Kramer was reporting directly to Singleton. Perhaps Kramer would be reluctant to talk to him directly, so he hoped Baker would be able to fill him in.

"Kramer met with Dr. Jenkins yesterday to discuss the findings of the autopsy and anything else he might be able to find out. We are supposed to meet in a couple of days to review where we stand with the investigation."

"Let me know what you find out after you meet with Kramer. I want to be kept well informed." Bacardi was concerned about the wrath of the attorney general if some surprise cropped up in the investigation. It was important that the department stay ahead of the curve should anything unexpected materialize.

"I think I may as well start by talking to Kendall first. Do you think you can call her and tell her that I am coming over to interview her? It will help if it came from you." Baker was anxious to get things moving.

"Sure. I will call her right now." Bacardi picked up the phone, dialed Kendall's number, and when he heard her voice, spoke into the mouthpiece.

"Sylvia. Good to talk to you. Listen, I have Morgan Baker here. He is investigating the death of the woman at Camp David on our behalf. He would like to come over and talk to you and get your insight on what might have happened." He sounded charming.

"Does he have to come over right now? I am in the middle of something," was Kendall's reply.

"You are always in the middle of something," Bacardi said snidely. "I would not expect anything else from you, Sylvia. That is your job, is it not? You are always involved in something. In fact, you are quite a busy young lady, aren't you? Yes, it is important that he sees you right away."

Kendall replied, "Okay. Let's say in about an hour?" and she hung up the phone before Bacardi could argue.

"She will see you in about an hour," Bacardi informed Baker as he watched him grabbing his hat and heading for the door. "Do you know where her office is?"

"Yes, I am sure I will find it."

"Great!" No point arguing with him.

As they shook hands, Bacardi added, "And be gentle with her, will you? She is a nice lady who was simply doing her job," to which Baker did not reply. Instead, he turned and left without even saying good-bye.

Chapter 28

IT WAS A mild summer's day, so Baker decided to walk to the social secretary's office, carrying his jacket over his right shoulder. With his coat off and his hat on, he felt comfortable enough for a midday stroll. He planned to see for himself the security procedures that were in place at the East Gate of the White House and to evaluate them as he entered the building. Presumably, the same security procedures would have been in place on the evening of the Fourth of July.

The office of the attorney general at the US Department of Justice is located at 950 Pennsylvania Avenue, Northwest, in Washington, DC, a short seven blocks from the White House where the office of the social secretary is located.

Having an hour to kill before his meeting with Kendall, Baker walked on Pennsylvania Avenue, admiring the shops along the way. He stopped for a short break at the United States Navy Memorial at 701 Pennsylvania Avenue to hear the concert being played there by the navy band. Government employees gathered around the Memorial to eat their lunch and to listen to the music.

By the time Baker arrived at the East Gate of the White House, his white shirt was drenched with perspiration. Although it was a fairly balmy day, he perspired profusely, something he was not able to control no matter how hard he tried. It was a battle that he lost more often than he cared to remember.

Standing across the street from the East Gate, he looked at the four corners of the street for any police surveillance cameras that would be helpful to the investigation. He was specifically interested in cameras that were pointed in the direction of the East Gate and that would have captured the comings and goings of guests as they entered or exited the White House. He saw at least two cameras pointing in that direction. He made a mental note to have the film from those cameras retrieved and examined as quickly as possible.

He crossed the street and went to the East Gate. The officer at the gate stopped Baker and asked to see his identification and to describe the purpose of his visit. Baker replied that he had an appointment with Sylvia Kendall and provided his private investigator's identification card as proof.

"It is not a very good likeness of me," he said to the guard who glanced several times at the photo then up at Baker until he was satisfied that indeed Baker was the same person who was in the photo. The guard asked Baker to wait while he called the secretary's office to confirm their appointment. Having done so, he allowed Baker to proceed to his meeting with Kendall. *Fairly straightforward*, Baker thought. *Nothing unusual so far.*

When he arrived at Kendall's office, she was ready for him with an outstretched hand and a big smile. Kendall looked very professional in her dark business suit as it was very becoming and well-tailored. The hemline of her skirt was slightly above her knee, not too high yet not too low either, Baker noted. The top two buttons of her white blouse were open, which allowed Baker a look at her hidden gems without being obvious about it.

"Hi. I am Sylvia Kendall." She shook Baker's hand and, like others, recoiled at the sweat that filled her palm. *Boy, this man sweats like a pig*, she thought then added sweetly, "What can I do for you?"

"I am Morgan Baker, private investigator for the Justice Department. May we sit down?" Baker wanted to get right down to business. "I am sure you heard about the body that was discovered at Camp David after the social event that, I believe, you had a major part in organizing." Baker looked at Kendall for a reaction but saw no hint that she knew what he was talking about. Baker thought it was just an act.

"Yes. That was a White House–sponsored event," she replied as they sat down. "All social events held by the White House are organized by this office." Her expression did not change as she stared at Baker, waiting for him to continue. Kendall was anxious to get back to her desk. Her workload was keeping her quite busy lately as there were many events to be managed prior to the upcoming election, including planning for the inauguration ceremonies.

"I was wondering if you could provide me with any information that might be helpful to the investigation of the woman's death at Camp David," Baker asked.

"I would be glad to help if I can," she replied. "What sort of information did you have in mind?"

Baker hoped that Kendall would be forthcoming and that he would not have to pull teeth. After all, he was a private investigator, not a dentist. He was investigating, on behalf of the Justice Department, a suspicious death that occurred at a White House–sponsored social event, and the more forthcoming Kendall was, the faster he would be gone from her office and out of her life.

"Let's start at the beginning, shall we? Tell me about the guest list. How was it prepared? How many guests were there, so forth and so on." Baker started the ball rolling.

"Well, let me see," Kendall sat back in her chair, crossed her legs and frowned. Baker noticed that she had beautiful legs and that she was wearing sheer nude stockings. "There are many considerations involved when preparing a guest list for a White House social event. There are certain people you always have to invite, such as the majority and minority leaders of both parties. Then, of course, you have to invite any foreign ambassadors or dignitaries who may be in town. But after that, we invite members of the business and entertainment community who were longtime supporters of the president as well as various political supporters and donors. And if we still have room on the guest list, we invite personal friends of the president and her husband."

"And how many were on the invitation list for this event who actually attended?" Baker needed a head count so he could follow up with them about their experience at the event.

"We had two hundred guests attending," Kendall quickly replied. "That was the magic number, two hundred," she repeated. She was pleased with herself and was happy to show it.

"Was that the total number of people who attended, including the president and vice president?" Baker asked.

"Oh no, no. It did not include the president and her husband or the vice president. So I suppose that would make it two hundred and three people who actually attended the festivities," Kendall was uneasy about Baker's line of questioning then added quickly, "in total."

"So if I understand you correctly," Baker went on, "there were a total of two hundred and three people who attended the event, besides waiters and support staff, is that correct?"

"Yes." Kendall was now suspicious of Baker as she sat facing him. She had to be more careful with her answers.

"And how do you know that the two hundred and three people who attended the festivities were the people you actually invited?" Baker's investigative experience told him to go slowly with his questioning at the beginning then to zoom in for the kill. He was nearly ready to nail Kendall.

Kendall sat up in her chair. "Because the identification card of each person who attended the function was examined at the East Gate and their name was checked off a master list of invitees that was prepared by this office before he or she was allowed to enter the White House." She was very proud of herself, and a smile appeared on her face. "I stood right at the East Gate, next to the guard, and looked over his shoulder to ensure that no one entered the White House who was not properly identified. They had to be on the master guest list."

"And that included wives and guests?"

"Of course!" Kendall beamed.

"Did you personally know everybody who was invited?" Baker was almost ready for the kill.

"No, of course not. I recognized many of them because they are well-known in political circles or in the industry or the entertainment world, but there was no way for me to recognize everybody who was invited or their wives and guests." Kendall did not know what Baker was driving at, and she had a funny expression on her face.

"But they all passed the test, right? It did not matter who they were. They were all identified with a picture identification card, which they produced at the gate and then were checked off the official guest list before they were allowed to enter the White House."

"Yes. That is right." Kendall was getting a bit annoyed with Baker. He was asking all these questions, the answers to which were fairly obvious and straightforward, she thought. *Is that why he is here? To take me away from my busy schedule with these stupid questions?*

"And that included the president and her husband as well as the vice president and his guest, right?"

"Well, no, that is not right." Kendall was getting upset. "We all know the president and her husband and the vice president, so we only had to check the identity of the vice president's guest."

"So you did not check the identities of the president, her husband, or of the vice president because you already knew and recognized them. I see." Baker thought about that for a moment. "But you said a minute ago that you also recognized many of the invited guests, but you checked their identity just the same. Is that not a bit of a contradiction?"

Kendal thought about that for a moment. "I suppose you might say that. But I would think that the president, her husband, and the vice president are in a different category than the other invited guests. I mean, if anything, they were the hosts of the event. Why would I need to check their identity when they were the hosts?" She paused for a moment. "Besides, they already were in the White House, so there was no need to check their identities. They were not at the East Gate. They were in the White House." Kendall pulled her shoulders back, beaming with confidence at her response. She thought that Baker posed a trick question and that she passed the test with flying colors.

"Good point, good point." Baker gave in. "They were already in the White House, so there was no need to check their identities," he repeated.

"But you did check the identity of the vice president's guest before she entered the White House, right?"

"I am sure we did." Kendall hoped that the questioning was nearly over.

"Okay, good." Baker thought about that a bit. "So just so I am clear. Of the two hundred and three people who attended the event, you only checked the identities of the two hundred invited guests who came through the East Gate, right?"

"Yes, that is right."

"All right, then. Let us talk now about what happened after the reception and dinner, when the guests were boarding the buses to go to Camp David."

"What do you mean?" Kendall seemed perplexed.

"Did you check the identities when everybody who was in the White House boarded the buses?"

"No, of course not. Why would we do that? There was no need to do that." She thought it was a stupid question.

"And why not? Why was there no need?" Baker was not giving up.

"Because their identities were already checked at the gate, before they entered the White House. Once they were in the White House, they were all together at the reception and dinner. There was no need to check their identities again, now was there?"

"And as far as you know, nobody left the building or exited the grounds only to return later because I assume if that happened, their identity would have been checked again, right?"

"Yes, for sure. As far as I know, and I am sure I am right, nobody left the building. But had they done so and would have wanted to return, their identity would have been checked again by the guard at the East Gate."

"Okay. So nobody left the White House, and now they were all boarding the buses, but their identities were not checked again because they were checked before." Baker considered that for a moment.

"Correct," Kendall brightened up, "but I personally counted all the people on each bus to ensure that only two hundred people were on the buses that were going to Camp David."

"And the president, her husband, and the vice president, I assume they all went by limousine, so that made it two hundred and three?" Baker did not wait for an answer. "Okay. That seems reasonable." He pondered that for a moment and added, "So the vice president's guest went on the bus also? She did not go with the vice president in the limousine?" He looked a little surprised.

"No, she was on the bus. There was one limo for the president, her husband, and the vice president. Nobody else was in that limousine. All two hundred of the invited guests, including the vice president's guest, were on the buses."

"And I assume that the next morning, when the festivities were over and everybody left Camp David that you counted bodies, I mean counted people again and that besides the president, her husband, and the vice president, there were one hundred and ninety nine people on the buses, since one guest died, right?"

"No, actually that is not right. I did not count the people leaving Camp David."

"No? Why not?" Baker was astounded.

"Because the event was over, and they were all leaving the camp. They were not arriving at the camp. They were leaving. There was no need to count them again as they exited. They were all leaving."

"Well, what about if, hypothetically, somebody decided to stay behind? How would you have known that someone stayed behind if you did not count the people on the way out and notice that you were missing one person?"

"That is a good point. I did not think about that. However, all the attendees were extensively vetted before they were invited, so there was no reason to suspect any of them of causing any mischief. This was a very select group of people who was invited, Mr. Baker. We are not talking about every Tom, Dick, and Harry."

It all seemed fair enough, and neat, which was what Baker feared the most. Based on his experience, he knew that when things were all tidy and neat, that was the time you really had to worry because things were not always what they appeared to be. Nevertheless, for now, he found no reason to be concerned with the identification procedures instituted by Kendall, although they were some obvious shortcomings.

"What about the event itself? Did anything unusual happen? Did anybody misbehave? Was there any hanky-panky going on that you were aware of or heard about?"

"Hanky-panky?" Lines appeared on Kendall's forehead as she raised her eyebrows. "Well, maybe some hanky, but certainly no panky." She laughed at her joke. Baker was not amused.

"What do you mean?" He said with a straight face.

"I was only kidding," Kendall was still laughing at her own joke.

"This is not a laughing matter," Baker admonished Kendall. "Somebody died under very mysterious circumstances, and let me remind you, Ms. Kendall, it was under your watch. It is my job to help find out how it happened and who, if anybody, was involved in this woman's death. I do not think that somebody dying at Camp David or at any time or any place for that matter is something to joke about."

"I am sorry. You are right. It is not a laughing matter. No, I did not see or hear anything unusual either at Camp David or at the White House."

Baker flipped through his notes. "Only a couple of more questions, Ms. Kendall, and then we will be done."

"Okay."

"Do you know who the dead woman was?"

"No, I do not. I only know what they said in the media, which is not much."

"And what is that? What did they say?"

"That she was a woman in her forties. That is all I know."

"In fact, Ms. Kendall, you do not know if the woman was one of your invited guests or not, do you?" Baker did not wait for a reply. "Because as you said, you did not know everybody by sight. She could have been one of the two hundred guests who came to Camp David on the bus, or possibly not. You have no way of knowing that, do you, since you did not count the people on the way out to know if one person was missing? I suppose it was possible that she came to the camp some other way, but I do not think that would have been very likely, considering the tight security at the camp and the way she was dressed, which was consistent with having attended the party." Baker was angry, and it showed.

Kendall quickly chimed in, "Let me stop you there for a moment, Mr. Baker. Actually, when I heard about the death on the radio, I contacted all the women who attended the event, and they all arrived safely home. So I do not think the woman who died at the camp was one of our invited guests."

That is very strange, Baker thought. *Very strange indeed.*

"Tell me, Ms. Kendall," Baker changed the subject. "If hypothetically, this woman who died at Camp David, if she was a lesbian, would she have been invited to the event? Would she have been able to attend?"

"I do not think there would have been any way for us to have known in advance that she was a lesbian, but if we knew, it would not have made a difference. She still would have been invited and would have been able to attend. That was not one of the criteria we used for disqualifying a person from attending the event."

"What about if she was a transgender, would that have made any difference to you at all?"

Kendall never faced this sort of a situation before, so she did not know how to answer. "I suppose we would have considered that in our decision, but I do not know how we would have known that in advance or what the decision would have been. However, I have no reason to think that it would have disqualified her from attending the event. The White House does not discriminate on the basis of race or gender or anything else for that matter." She wondered why Baker was asking her all these questions that had nothing to do with the real issue, which was how and why a woman died at Camp David after a White House–sponsored event.

"All right, then. That will be all for now. I may need to talk to you again, but for now, if you could please provide me with a copy of the guest list." Kendall answered all of Baker's questions, and he was ready to leave. She rushed off to a file cabinet somewhere in the adjoining room and, a few minutes later, returned with a copy of the guest list in a manila envelope.

"Here is a list of everybody who attended the event." She stood up and stretched her hand to Baker, who got the message that the meeting was over and he was being dismissed. He stood up and shook her hand. This time, however, Kendall was prepared. She wore white gloves. Baker did not know what to make of it.

"Thank you for seeing me on such short notice. Good-bye." He turned and left.

Standing at the doorway for a minute longer, Kendall wondered which shoe was going to fall next. The celebratory event was supposed to be a happy event and, instead, wound up nearly a complete disaster with several unanswered questions remaining and an unidentified corpse. That was not what was supposed to happen. It reflected badly on the social office.

Chapter 29

IT WAS ALREADY the third week of July, and the opening ceremony of the summer Olympics in Tel Aviv, Israel, was ready to begin. Israel's security forces with Uzis in hand were everywhere—at airports, bus stops, and at all major intersections. Israel promised that the Olympics was going to be a peaceful international contest of athletic prowess, and it aimed to fulfill its promise.

In Washington, DC, however, where promises were rarely kept and chance sometimes played a greater role than performance, a political firestorm was brewing. The story of the death of a woman at Camp David after a White House–sponsored event was on everyone's lips and was gaining momentum. Social media picked up the story and, unencumbered by journalistic oversight, embellished it with rumors and innuendo. By the time the public got the news on their desktop computers and smartphones, truth and fiction were so intertwined that it was left with a version that was far from reality and completely unrecognizable by those directly involved in the investigation.

"I met with Bacardi," Baker began, "and he promised to look into getting better cooperation from the commander at Camp David. He also agreed to provide me with copies of the videos around the White House. As for the videos at Camp David, I am sure that will take a little more prodding, but I am hopeful that eventually, they will come around and supply us with what we need to solve this investigation."

They were sitting in Kramer's office, surrounded by boxes full of paperwork representing different cases. The number of cases that Kramer was working on increased substantially since he became embroiled in the Camp David investigation.

His hands behind his head, Kramer sat at his desk, leaning precariously backward until his head nearly touched the bookcase behind him. His desktop computer partially obscured his vision of Baker, who sat across the desk, barely fitting into the arm chair, his massive frame overtaking any available space. The man was huge!

"Okay, but did you find out anything at all since we last met?"

Baker told Kramer how he met with Kendall, the White House social secretary. "It was a very interesting and informative meeting," he said. "Apparently, by her count, two hundred guests entered the White House and two hundred people boarded the buses to Camp David. She never counted the number of people leaving Camp David, although she verified after the event that all the women who attended the party returned home safely."

"I find that very strange," he continued, "because we now have a woman who died at Camp David, but who may not have been one of the invited guests. This is hard for me to imagine considering the tight security at the camp. As far as I can tell, the likelihood that somebody could sneak into the camp or be brought there by one of the military troops without being detected is close to zero."

"I tend to agree with you," Kramer chimed in. "I cannot see how anybody would have been able to do that, although I suppose where there is a will there is a way."

"Actually, in my opinion, where there is a will, there is a body," Baker corrected Kramer. It was a bit of humor that he interjected into a day that had nothing funny about it. Kramer had difficulty picturing Baker as a stand-up comic.

Kramer was puzzled. They were working the investigation for some time now, and they needed a break. "Something is not right, and I think it is staring us right in the face, but we don't recognize it."

"How about you? Did you find out anything more?" It was Baker who was asking the questions now.

"Yeah, I did. Hear this," Kramer tried to stretch the moment. "I met with Dr. Jenkins. As you know, the dead woman was a transgender. Interestingly, Jenkins extracted a small round undigested blue pill from her stomach that I will try to identify. However, if she had an undigested pill in her stomach, there is a good chance that she took more drugs that entered her blood before she died and would be picked up in the drug analysis. I need the toxicology report to confirm that. More importantly, it will tell us whether the amount of drug in her system was at an overdose level.

"Anything else?"

"No, not yet. I am waiting for Jenkins to provide me with the autopsy and toxicology reports. I am sure they will be very helpful in answering many of the questions that we still have, including how the woman died."

"I find it interesting that there still has not been a missing person report for this woman." It was Baker now. "Maybe it is because she was a transgender and people do not want to be publicly associated with her. I will see if Bacardi would be willing to put out a reward for information. But the more I think about it, the more I think that he probably would not want to do that since they want to keep this whole incident quiet. Needless to say, it makes my job more difficult if I cannot identify the body."

"Well, when we find out exactly what happened, we might find out who this woman was." Kramer had a feeling that everything would fall into place when all the pieces of the puzzle were identified.

"I am going to check with Bacardi to see if the surveillance videos near the White House are available. I think that they should be easier to obtain than videos taken at Camp David. Once I get them, we can view them together."

"Good. In the meantime, I will prod Jenkins to hurry the process along and to at least get me drafts of the autopsy and toxicology reports if the final reports are not yet available. They should help clarify the situation." Kramer was counting on it.

Chapter 30

IF EVER A Republican National Convention was to be called a spectacle, this year's convention would surely rank as the one most deserving of the label. Held in the nation's capital, it promised to provide high-wire acts, jugglers, elephants, and equally important, drama, intrigue, and suspense. It would not disappoint.

Washington, DC, is a great convention town with its 2.3 million square foot Walter E. Washington Convention Center, many high-end hotels, including the Ritz-Carlton, the Park Hyatt, and the Four Seasons, and numerous five-star restaurants.

After careful consideration of all the available space, the Republicans chose to anoint their candidate for the highest office in the land at the Washington Hilton Hotel, the same venue where Ronald Reagan, their idol and political mascot, was shot on March 30, 1981, by John Hinckley Jr. Selecting the Hilton, a place where a Republican president nearly died, might have been an omen of things to come, for there were many signs that the demise of the Republican Party was nearly here.

The second week of August saw the population of the Republicans in Washington, DC, exploding while the resident Democrats escaped the oppressive and humid Washington weather for the coolness of Colorado. That was the location where the Democratic National Convention was scheduled to be held in early September.

Colorado in August is a wonderful place to visit. Aspen and Vale are colorful towns with art galleries and restaurants catering to tourists. The views of the mountains and valleys are unlike anything that can be seen elsewhere in the United States, certainly not on the East Coast, where high-rise buildings and industrial sites dominate the mid-Atlantic skyline.

As the Republican National Convention got under way, it appeared that it would definitely live up to its promises. Political operatives juggled while delegates performed high-wire acts, balancing fact and fiction with the greatest of ease. Tewkesbury did his magic act as he made deals, split hairs, and cajoled delegates. There were elephants in the room, of course, for it would be un-American to have a Republican National Convention without elephants. But drama, intrigue, and suspense were reserved for the last night of the convention when Slocum would arrive after four days of wheeling, dealing, and conniving in the back rooms of the hotel to announce his pick of a vice presidential running mate. At the appropriate moment, balloons and confetti would come streaming down from the rafters, and a video of the two candidates would be shown on a jumbotron inside the convention hall and on a giant screen outside the hotel, overlooking the world-famous Connecticut Avenue. No one would dare deny that an event such as the one being organized by the Republicans would not deserve being mentioned in the *Guinness Book of Records* as a spectacle extraordinaire. That simply would be unthinkable!

On the morning of the last day of the convention, Slocum was in his room, uneasy as he was badly trailing his Democratic opponent. The death of the woman at Camp David after the White House–sponsored event had little effect on the Worthing-Bunting lead. He did not understand why there was no movement in his standing in the polls, but he could not dwell on it either. He had to choose a running mate who would catapult him to a comfortable lead on the road to the White House in November. But who?

There was no shortage of advice from various Republican had-beens on whom to select, but Slocum was not listening to any of them. He was not about to choose any of their recommendations. That was a sure way to lose the election, he thought. No, Slocum was going to choose a totally fresh face, maybe one from the political world or perhaps somebody from the business world. He did not decide yet, but his choice would definitely shake things up. Of course, John McCain tried to do that by selecting Sarah Palin to be his running mate. That turned out to be a complete disaster. Slocum was determined not to make the same mistake that McCain did.

While Slocum was contemplating his choices of a running mate, Kramer was working in his office, trying to go through the papers on his desk and reduce the clutter in his office. At precisely two o'clock that afternoon, his phone rang. It was Jennifer Sweet on the line.

"What a pleasant surprise." Kramer turned on the speakerphone as he examined medical records for one of his medical malpractice cases, his eyes gleaming with excitement. "Are you in town? When can I see you again?"

"I will be landing in DC at about five o'clock for an overnight stay and was hoping you would like to get together," Sweet said and held her breath, hoping that Kramer was free on such short notice. She was thinking about him ever since Bunting dumped her. She thought that now was a perfect time to begin a new relationship with an interesting and intriguing man, probably more interesting that Bunting was.

"I was wondering when I would see you again." Kramer put on his golden charm. Sweet noticed that Kramer said when and not if he would see her again. "I would love to get together and spend the night with you," he added. "I'll tell you what," he continued. "Can you meet me at 1789 in Georgetown, let's say, at seven o'clock? We can have a nice, quiet dinner then go to my place and watch Slocum's acceptance speech at the Republican National Convention. It should be quite a night, I am sure of it." Kramer meant that remark in more ways than one.

"That sounds lovely." Sweet was excited with the evening's prospects. She picked up on Kramer's meaning. "I will see you at seven," she said and hung up the phone.

Kramer was delighted to hear from Sweet and stopped rearranging the papers on his desk and reclined in his chair. As he was accustomed to doing when thinking deep thoughts, he crossed his hands behind his head and closed his eyes. He let his mind conjure all sorts of sexually explicit moments with Jennifer Sweet. A smile came across his lips as his heart raced and his excitement escalated at the thought of seeing Sweet again. He opened his eyes and tried to shake the pornographic images from his mind. There would be plenty of time later to put his thoughts into action, but for now, he had to concentrate on the cases that were stacked on his desk and all over his office floor. They required his full attention.

After her phone conversation with Kramer, Sweet went to the airport to catch the American Airlines flight to DC. Although she was working the flight, her mind was elsewhere. Thankfully, the flight was uneventful with no unexpected emergencies that would have necessitated her complete attention. She was a professional and would have risen to the task if an emergency actually occurred. However, she was not as focused on her job that day as she usually was, in part because she was still recovering emotionally from being recently dumped by Bunting. Seeing Kramer again and beginning a new relationship was her way of mending her broken heart and getting back in the saddle again. She laughed when she thought of the phrase "get back in the saddle again."

"I think I will ride Kramer tonight, ride him, but good." She laughed at the thought.

A quarter to seven that evening found Kramer sitting at a table for two on the second floor of the 1789 Restaurant located on Thirty-Sixth Street, Northwest. in

Georgetown. It was one of his favorite French restaurants with delicious food and waiters who were efficient but unobtrusive. It was the perfect place to meet a delectable vision like Jennifer Sweet. He ordered a bottle of Pinot Noir, had the waiter pour him a glass, and waited patiently for Sweet to make her entrance.

As if on cue, all eyes turned to the doorway as the clock struck seven and Jennifer entered wearing a black skintight dress that accentuated her well-proportioned figure. With her long blond hair cascading down to her shoulders and her painted lips glowing in the dim candlelit room, Sweet was a sight that was not lost on the men seated in the room. All wanted to know who the lucky man was who would bed her that night. Little did they expect to find that it would be a fifty-something-year-old man with a small and unbecoming mustache and a slight paunch around his midriff. When they did, their look of amazement was reflected on the faces of their wives and girlfriends.

Jennifer's smile was as wide as the river Nile when she saw Kramer seated by the window, looking in her direction. He got out of his chair as she approached, kissed her sweetly on the cheek, and pulled her chair away from the table as she sat down. Placing her Christian Dior black clutch to the side, Sweet looked across the table at Kramer, who was busy pouring her a glass of the red wine he had ordered earlier. They raised and clicked their glasses and sipped the vintage brew while gazing into each other's eyes over the candlelight.

"Mm, delicious. Just what I needed. What year was that?" She was getting into the mood after a long day."Pinot Noir, 2012," Kramer responded with aplomb. "It was a wonderful year for wine, so I am glad you like it." He took another sip. She was right. It was delicious. "So glad to see you again." He reached across the table and held her hands. They were well manicured, warm, and soft. Sweet let him hold her, noting that his fingers were smoother than she expected.

"Yeah, it's been a long time since I saw you last, so when I found out that I was going to be in town, I thought it would be a great chance to reconnect."

"I am glad you did." He gave her hands a squeeze. "Shall we order?"

Sweet selected the summer melon salad, followed by the wild Alaska king salmon for her main course. Kramer chose the chilled corn chowder as a starter and the breast of duck (he was partial to breast) with pistachio foie gras truffle, rainbow beets, summer berries, and Valrhona chocolate for his entrée. For dessert, they shared the almond crème brûlée, a house specialty and a longtime favorite of his.

It was not long thereafter that Sweet and Kramer found themselves in Kramer's apartment, sharing his king-size bed and making mad love while the television blared in the background with speeches from the Republican National Convention. Sweet's beauty intoxicated Kramer as he relished in the curvature of her breasts and hips, the smoothness of her skin, and the sweetness of her lips. He was aroused by her every kiss, his senses heightened by the aroma of her perfume. *This surely is heaven on earth*, Kramer thought as he made love to Sweet. He embraced the moment and aimed to make it last. Alas, Kramer could not last long, for Sweet was much too exciting for him to be able to hold back the explosive nature of his manhood. He let out a loud "Oh god" as he climaxed then rolled over, exhausted.

Sweet was enthralled by the energy with which Kramer went about making love to her. She wondered which god was responsible for Kramer's sexual stamina and generosity. *Quite a tiger*, she thought, *and much better in bed than Bunting ever was, that's for sure.* She was glad that Kramer was happy to see her and hoped that this new relationship would flourish. *Who needs Bunting?* she concluded. She let the thought out of her head and concentrated on satisfying Kramer. *He certainly knows how to kiss, and his smooth fingers are able to find my most sensitive arousal points.* With that thought swirling in her head, she experienced an orgasm the likes of which she never experienced before. "Oh, please, more, *please*," she whispered in Kramer's ear. With a sigh and a heave, she settled her head back on the pillow, completely spent.

The speeches at the Republican National Convention seemed to go on forever as Sweet and Kramer lay back, resting after their intense lovemaking. It is at this point, at least in the 1950s, when they would have smoked a Marlboro cigarette and had a drink of wine or scotch. But this was the twenty-first century, and smoking and drinking were frowned upon, so instead, they lay back and looked at the ceiling, noticing cracks above their heads that needed repair.

At the convention hall, it was nearly time for Slocum to arrive and deliver his acceptance speech. There was an air of anticipation as the four-day convention was nearly at its end. All the delegates wanted to know who Slocum picked as his vice presidential running mate.

Rested and recovered from their passionate lovemaking, Kramer reached over and mounted Sweet again. She did not resist. He kissed her tenderly on the lips then nibbled on her right ear. "You are so delicious," he said, sucking her earlobe. She let out a small giggle and hugged Kramer. "Am I really?"

"Yes, you are." He nibbled at her left ear now to make them even.

The loud applause at the convention hall when Slocum entered the room did not interfere with Kramer and Sweet's vigorous lovemaking. Kramer kept his ears on the telecast, but his eyes were on Sweet as their lovemaking intensified.

"My fellow Republicans, I am honored to be here tonight as your nominee for president of the United States." A loud cheer filled the convention floor as the Republicans rejoiced, hoping that this was the year of the elephant.

"You are a much better lover than my previous boyfriend." Sweet could not help herself. She felt Kramer cupping his hands around her breasts as he kissed her cheeks with butterfly kisses. "You definitely know how to push my buttons."

Kramer wished the moment would never end. It was total bliss, and he was in seventh heaven. "Am I?" He asked and kissed her breasts and sucked her nipples. "And who was your last boyfriend?" he asked between kisses as he methodically explored Sweet's body, leaving no crevice untouched. "Anybody I know?"

"You wouldn't believe me if I told you." Sweet loved making love with Kramer. He was so generous and giving. She wished it would go on forever.

"Try me." Kramer was curious, and he looked at Sweet, unable to guess who it was and why she had another boyfriend when she should have had him all along.

In the background, the telecast of the Republican National Convention was now in full swing. *"I come to you tonight as your nominee and the American people's humble servant with the specific purpose of giving our country back to its rightful owners—your every day, common American."* Another thunderous applause, even louder than before.

"Eric Bunting." Sweet blurted out with pride.

Abruptly stopping what he was doing, Kramer raised his head and looked at Jennifer Sweet. "Do you mean Eric Bunting, the vice president of the United States? Is that what you are telling me?" he asked in disbelief. "Bunting was your previous boyfriend?"

"Yes, one and the same. I knew you would never believe me," she answered and pulled him closer.

"Well, if that is what you are telling me, then I guess I believe you, but it is hard for me to imagine it. How long was it going on?" Kramer nibbled on her nipples again, letting his hands explore her body and finding new areas that he did not touch before.

Sweet had her eyes closed, enjoying the foreplay. "Just a couple of months," she answered coyly. She was in ecstasy. "But we had an argument at the Fourth of July celebration, and he broke it off that night," she added. "I was devastated, of course, but you gotta move on, you know?"

Having an argument with a woman is not a problem, Kramer thought, *if having makeup sex is its reward.* He turned to Sweet and asked incredulously, "Are you telling me that you were at the White House event? The Fourth of July celebration?"

"I was only at the White House for the dinner and fireworks. I never went to Camp David," she replied.

"Let me see if I understand you correctly." He sat up in bed and was completely focused now. "You were at the White House that night, on the Fourth of July, but you did not go to Camp David?"

"That's right. We had an argument when we were watching the fireworks in the Rose Garden. He broke it off, and I never got a chance to get on the bus. Why, what's wrong?" Sweet tried to pull Kramer closer, but his body tensed, and he was not responding.

"Oh my god! I need to make a phone call." He got out of bed and completely naked, walked over to the desk, picked up the phone, and dialed Baker's number. When he heard Baker's voice, he said, "We need to talk. Did you get the videos at the White House gate yet?"

"I got them today," Baker responded.

"Good. Let's look at them together in the morning. Come to my office at 9:00 a.m. I think I know what happened." He hung up.

The television was still broadcasting the Republican National Convention. Slocum was nearly at the point in his speech when he would announce his selection of his vice presidential running mate. *"I want to introduce to you the next vice president of the United States"*—his speech was nearly over—*"Jeremiah Jackson."*

A tall, slender African American Republican senator from Mississippi walked up to the platform and embraced Slocum with a wide grin, and the two men clasped hands and held them high in the air. The roar of the crowd washed over them as the delegate-filled auditorium cheered for what seemed like an eternity. Balloons came down from the rafters, streamers floated every which way, and the place went wild with excitement.

Chapter 31

"JENNIFER SWEET, THE vice president's date at the Fourth of July White House party, she never went to Camp David."

"What do you mean?" Baker did not understand what Kramer was trying to say.

"Exactly what I said. She went to the White House for the reception and dinner but never boarded the bus to Camp David." Kramer's voice rose as his excitement mounted.

"That is impossible," Baker replied. "Kendall counted two hundred people on the buses who went to Camp David. What makes you say a stupid thing like that?"

"I also thought it was impossible, but that is what she told me, and I believe her."

"Jennifer Sweet told you that? When?"

Kramer thought that Baker was slow to comprehend. "Last night, when we were making love." He turned so Baker would not see the amused expression on his face.

Baker did not want to hear about Kramer's evening with Jennifer Sweet, which he was sure would be filled with many juicy and titillating tidbits. He sensed that there was an interesting man-to-man story there that he would love to hear about under different circumstances, but he did not have time for that now. They had a mysterious death to solve. He would stay focused on solving the cause of the woman's death at Camp David.

"Did you bring the tapes?" Kramer asked. "I think they should provide at least part of the answer to what happened that night." Kramer was anxious to begin viewing the tapes.

"I transferred them to six CDs, each about thirty minutes long, so it will take about three hours to see all of them."

"Then we better get started." Kramer was anxious to begin watching the CDs. If he was right, they should confirm his suspicion of what happened that night. "I have the CD player hooked up to the television, so we might as well begin. Hopefully, we should finish viewing all the CDs before lunch." He put the first CD into the CD player and pressed the Play button on the remote. Soon, images of the street corner in front of the White House appeared on the screen.

Looking for a place to sit, Baker saw only armchairs in Kramer's office. He could barely squeeze his massive frame into one of those chairs. Kramer thought that Baker really needed to lose weight, but it wasn't his place to tell him. He was constantly fighting his own battle of the bulge. Nevertheless, being a biological scientist, he thought that at the rate Baker was going, it would be only a matter of time before he would come down with congestive heart failure or diabetes.

Baker was sweating profusely, and it was only nine o'clock in the morning. Kramer thought that if the opportunity arose, he would suggest to Baker that he should have a complete physical examination.

Taking off his crumpled hat and placing it in a small clearing at the right corner of Kramer's desk, Baker tried his best to make himself comfortable in the armchair as he sat opposite Kramer. Kramer's eyes were glued to the monitor, looking for anything unusual. So far, he only saw pedestrians, cars, and a traffic light changing from green to yellow to red and then repeat the cycle ad nauseam. Thirty minutes later, they concluded that the camera did not capture anything unusual. They were ready to see the second CD.

Kramer hoped that viewing the second CD would be more productive. On this one, the camera captured images of guests as they lined up to enter the East Gate of the White House. Kramer and Baker stood up and walked closer to the TV screen to get a better view. Although the line was long, the procession seemed orderly, and the guests appeared calm as they proceeded toward the gate. Kramer saw the officer at the gate checking identification cards with Kendall standing to his right and slightly behind him, looking over his shoulder and checking the names against her master list of invitees. All seemed as it should be. Women chatted and giggled among themselves while the men held their arm and escorted them through the gate. Kramer recognized a few of the guests, but not many. He was not an avid follower of politicians or politics. There was not much daylight, and the streetlamps did not provide sufficient illumination, so many of the images captured by the camera were in darkness or blurred. Nevertheless, neither Baker nor Kramer saw anything amiss with the procedures at the East Gate.

After they finished viewing the second CD, they took a short break before watching the third CD. Kramer wondered if he was wrong. Maybe there was nothing on any of the CDs that would assist them with the investigation.

"What are we looking for?" Baker was getting anxious. So far, he watched for an hour and saw nothing that was helpful for the investigation. "You said you knew what happened."

"I need confirmation before I can tell you what I think," Kramer replied. "We only saw two CDs so far, and there are four more to go. Let's watch the remaining CDs before I tell you what I think happened."

They stood by the window and looked out. It felt good to stretch their legs. Baker especially was thankful because he felt like a sardine sitting in the armchair. Across the way, a Pepco truck was parked along the side of the road. An electrician climbed a nearby electric pole to repair the damage caused by a recent storm that passed through the area, causing havoc in some of the power lines. For some reason, power failures happened more frequently in the Maryland suburbs than elsewhere. Kramer hoped that this time, Pepco would fix the problem well enough so that it would not happen again during the next storm, but he was not sure if that was possible. Power failures seemed to be a normal part of life in Maryland.

"Shall we go ahead and watch the third one?" Kramer wanted to get started. It would soon be lunchtime.

"Sure, let's do it." Baker sat down again in the uncomfortable armchair, only this time, he took off his jacket and tie. It was going to be a long morning, so he might as well be comfortable.

Kramer put the next CD into the CD player, pressed the On button on the remote again, and sat back in his swivel chair behind his desk. Unlike Baker, he would be much more relaxed and comfortable as he put his feet up on the desk and stared at the TV monitor.

Neither the third nor fourth CDs provided any clues as to what happened on the night of the Fourth of July celebration. It was now past eleven o'clock, and Kramer and Baker were getting tired. On occasion, Baker would close his eyes and take cat naps. That their stomachs grumbled, it being nearly lunchtime, did not help. "We are almost done," Kramer said as he kicked Baker's chair to wake him up and casually placed the fifth CD into the CD player. "Let's try to finish watching these before lunch."

The fifth CD showed guests exiting through the front doors of the White House and walking toward the waiting buses. Because of the great distance between the surveillance cameras, which were set on the street, high above and close to the traffic light, and the White House main doors, it was difficult to recognize any faces when people stood in the doorway of the White House.

Also, since all the men wore tuxedos and, for all practical purposes, looked the same, it was nearly impossible to identify most of them. However, as the procession walked along the sidewalk and came nearer to the cameras, it became easier to identify some of the guests, although the lighting still was not ideal. The CD ran out just as the first few guests began boarding the buses. It was time to watch the final CD. Kramer reloaded the CD player with the last CD. Baker barely had his eyes open. Thankfully, he was not snoring. It would have been very embarrassing had he done so, Kramer thought.

The last CD picked up where the fifth one ended. This time, Kramer stood up again and positioned himself close to the TV screen for better viewing. *We better see something on this one*, he thought. Even Baker, now wide awake, repositioned his chair closer to the monitor and paid more attention to the final CD. Getting tapes from Camp David would be nearly impossible, so if there was any evidence on any of the CDs that would help the investigation, it better be on this one.

The hazy images were barely recognizable in the dim light. Kramer and Baker focused on the procession as it moved toward the waiting buses. Occasionally, they would recognize the face of one of the guests, but these were few and far between. They could hear the sounds of the National Symphony Orchestra playing in the background. A jovial atmosphere prevailed as the procession moved along, and all seemed orderly and without mishap. Kramer strained his eyes and tried to focus on the blurred images on the screen. Baker was now standing next to him, not wanting to miss anything important.

Then, unexpectedly, the loud sounds of cannons being fired could be heard. The procession immediately stopped, and everyone in line turned around toward the White House to better hear the cannons and see the exploding fireworks electrify the night sky. It was a moment not to be missed, for sure, but Kramer thought he saw some movement at the front of the line, near the bus, that seemed out of place. He immediately hit the Pause button on the remote.

"What? What is the matter?" Baker looked at Kramer questioningly.

"I think I saw something. I am going to rewind a bit and see if I can see it again. I want you to pay close attention also, and keep your eyes open for anything unusual."

More alert now, Baker moved even closer to the monitor so he could get a better view. After rewinding, Kramer pressed the Slow Motion button on the remote but kept his finger on the Pause button, just in case he had to stop the CD again. The images on the monitor began to move only this time; Baker watched more intently.

"Keep your eyes on the people at the front of the line as they get on the bus," Kramer told Baker. "Tell me if you see anything unusual or unexpected."

The procession moved very slowly when viewed in slow motion. All seemed normal. Kramer hit the Pause button for a moment. "If I am correct," he said, "this is Jennifer Sweet at the front of the line, ready to board the bus." He pointed at the image of Sweet as she momentarily turned around, looking at the fireworks. Her blond hair was in an updo, and she was wearing a powder-blue evening gown with her left shoulder fully exposed.

"Did you see her?" he asked Baker. "Did you see her?" he asked again. "She is wearing a blue evening gown that is very similar to the one that was worn by the woman who died at Camp David, the body that I saw at the morgue. Also, look here"—he pointed, zooming in on Sweet's face—"she has a beauty mark at the right corner of her mouth. Can you see that?" He turned to Baker, who nodded.

"So how does that help us?" Baker did not understand the point Kramer was trying to make.

"Wait a minute. You will see. There is more." Kramer pressed the Slow Motion button again, and the images began moving again. Baker even paid more attention this time, as if that were possible. The line stopped its forward movement as the cannons exploded and people turned toward the sound. In the darkness, Baker and Kramer saw all the guests looking backward at the fireworks with the exception of Sweet, who turned forward again, this time holding on to the railing of the bus, ready to board. Then, out of the shadows, an image of a man appeared to the right of Sweet with a woman trailing closely behind him. The woman bore a striking resemblance to Sweet and wore a blue gown that was very similar to the one worn by Sweet. As Sweet was about to board the bus, the man grabbed her right arm and pulled her away from the bus toward a waiting car, while the woman who was behind him took Sweet's place in line and boarded the bus.

"Did you see that?" Kramer asked incredulously. "Did you see that?" he asked again.

Baker's mouth was wide open in utter amazement. "You bet I did," he responded in disbelief. "No wonder Kendall was able to get a correct head count even though Jennifer Sweet never boarded the bus and did not go to Camp David."

"I will set up the CD again to make sure we did not miss anything."

They again watched only that portion of the CD where the switch was made. This time they knew exactly what to look for and where they should focus their attention. They saw Jennifer Sweet slowly reach the front of the line and about to raise her right leg and board the bus. Then, out of the darkness, they saw a man appear and grab Sweet's right arm and lead her to a waiting car. A woman who was trailing behind the man, who bore an uncanny resemblance to Sweet, took Sweet's place in the procession and boarded the bus. All this happened while everyone else had their backs toward the waiting bus and their eyes diverted toward the White House and the fireworks bursting overhead. This time, from their standing position close to the TV monitor, and zooming in on the woman's face, Kramer and Baker could see that like Sweet, the woman who boarded the bus also had a beauty mark at the corner of her mouth, only hers was at the left corner, whereas Sweet's was on the right. Baker perked up as this was an obvious error made by the impostor. It was just the kind of investigative work that he found fascinating. They sat back in their chairs aghast at what they saw.

"You know what that means?" It was Baker who spoke first as he looked at Kramer. He did not wait for an answer. "Somebody was playing dirty tricks that evening, and in my opinion, the vice president was involved up to his blue eyeballs in this."

Kramer had no doubt that Baker was right. Jennifer Sweet was the vice president's date at the event. That he did not mention her absence at Camp David meant that he was in on what they just witnessed and perhaps involved in the woman's death. This was beginning to get very sinister.

"And I will tell you another thing," Baker continued. "The woman you saw boarding the bus instead of Jennifer Sweet is none other than the woman whose body was found at Camp David the following morning beneath the oak tree."

"And we still don't know who she is, do we?" Kramer said to no one in particular.

Baker reached for his hat because he was ready to leave. "That was one of the surprises I had for you this morning," he replied as he put on his hat. He walked across the room to where his jacket lay draped over another armchair, took out a pad from the breast pocket, and read his notes. "Her name was Erica Brown, a well-known transgender from Washington, DC, who with a little makeup in all the right places and a blue gown transformed herself to the spitting image of Jennifer Sweet."

"The switch must have been planned very cunningly by someone close to the vice president for weeks, if not months in advance of the event," Baker added. "What we need to find out now is why it was done, who planned it, and who else was involved. And most importantly," he added, "how does it relate to the woman's death."

"Precisely," Kramer responded. "And I think I know how we are going to do exactly that."

Halfway out the door, Baker heard Kramer calling after him. "Wait a minute. You said that was one of the surprises you had for me. What was the other surprise?" Baker turned around. "Oh, I nearly forgot." He reached deep into his left pant pocket and pulled out a small plastic bag. "I think you were looking for this?" He said, smiling. The bag contained a long dangling yellow-gold earring with a pearl at the bottom that was made for pierced ears. It was the mate to the one Kramer had seen at the morgue, only this one had bloodstains on it.

"I had Bacardi arrange for a search warrant, and I went to Camp David again. I found this earring in the same room that the vice president occupied the night of the White House event. It was at the foot of the bed, hidden by the bedspread. I had the blood analyzed for DNA, and bingo. It was a perfect match for a transgender named Erica Brown. You already told me that the other earring was at the morgue. Now, what do you think about that?" Baker smiled at Kramer, who was standing in complete amazement. "You must admit that I am some detective, huh?"

Kramer hated to admit it, but he was beginning to like Baker. "I will touch base with you when I get the autopsy and toxicology reports," he told Baker as he continued to stare at the earring, but by then, Baker was already gone.

Chapter 32

KRAMER WAS IN front of his computer, trying to identify the pill that Jenkins found in the dead woman's stomach. He googled "pill identification" and found 1,960,000 postings in 0.38 seconds. He clicked on the first entry, "Pill Identification Wizard from Drugs.com," and began his search.

In the Imprint box, he typed M30, the markings that Jenkins said he found on the pill. For color, he selected Blue, and for shape, he picked Round. He clicked the Search button, and up came two possible choices for his search criteria. The first was a 30 milligram tablet of oxycodone hydrochloride, a narcotic medication manufactured by Mallinckrodt Pharmaceuticals. The second choice was a 3.75 milligram pill of clorazepate dipotassium, a sedative and anticonvulsant drug of the benzodiazepine class. He consulted his notes of his meeting with Jenkins and saw that Jenkins mentioned that the tablet was scored on one side, right below the number 30. The picture of an oxycodone hydrochloride tablet that appeared on Drugs.com perfectly matched Jenkins's description, whereas clorazepate dipotassium did not. "Definitely oxycodone hydrochloride," Kramer concluded, "a narcotic."

Now we are getting somewhere, he thought. He was making progress. An undigested 30 milligram oxycodone pill in the dead woman's stomach meant that she probably also had oxycodone in her blood at the time of her death. If the amount of the drug in her blood was sufficiently high, it could have led to her death. If true, the toxicology report would confirm that.

At four o'clock, FedEx arrived at Kramer's office and delivered a large cardboard Priority envelope. Trudy signed for the package and handed it to Kramer, who was still in front of his computer. He barely looked up when she handed him the envelope.

"What is that?" he asked, not looking up.

"Why don't you open it and find out?" she replied.

He looked at Trudy and grudgingly opened the envelope, expecting her to have opened it for him.

The envelope had a return address from the Medical Examiner's Office. He was all thumbs as he opened the cardboard envelope. Inside, he found another large manila envelope, through which he inserted a letter opener. With one quick motion, he tore it open. It contained copies of the draft autopsy and toxicology reports. So important were these documents that Kramer felt as if he was holding the Holy Grail and had to wear surgical gloves when handling them, lest they disintegrated right in front of his eyes. He decided to review the autopsy report first.

The top-right corner of the report was stamped DRAFT in big, bold letters, probably because a number of the items were unknown and missing. The name of the deceased was labeled Jane Doe, although Kramer knew that Baker identified the body as that of Erica Brown, a forty-three-year-old transgender from Washington, DC. Baker would share this information with the medical examiner, who, in due course, would update the information in the final version of the report.

The sections labeled Final Diagnoses, Opinion, Cause of Death, and Manner of Death were all identified as pending, most likely because Jenkins prepared the draft autopsy report before the draft toxicology report was available.

Reading an autopsy report was like reading an anatomical road map. By the time Kramer finished

245

reading the report, he was aware of the health of all the dead woman's major organs and identified all the relevant biological guideposts that would help explain any medical conditions from which she suffered.

The four-page report began with, "I hereby certify that I, Christopher Jenkins, MD, Maryland medical examiner, have performed an autopsy on the body of Jane Doe on the fifth day of July . . ." Sections labeled as External Examination, Internal Examination, Final Diagnoses, Opinion, Cause of Death, and Manner of Death followed thereafter. The last items in the report were Dr. Jenkins's signature and date, but the report was unsigned and undated because it was only a draft report.

In reviewing the report, Kramer was particularly struck by the condition of the body. It was well developed, well nourished, and consistent with that of a forty-year-old female. The external examination performed by Jenkins revealed evidence of genital reconstruction surgery, which Kramer already knew was one of the reasons why Jenkins concluded that the woman was a transgender.

Jenkins's examination of the internal organs showed that the woman had an enlarged heart that weighed 580 grams. This was much larger than the 250–350 grams weight of a normal human heart and was a risk factor for sudden death. Also, she had atherosclerosis with 50 percent narrowing of the aorta and 80 to 85 percent narrowing of both of her coronary arteries. Taken in total, these anatomical abnormalities led Kramer to conclude that the woman was a potential powder keg for a heart-related medical emergency, such as an arrhythmia or a heart attack, that at any time could have resulted in death.

Although her lungs were pink and healthy looking, they were mildly congested and oozing fluid, a sign that she had pulmonary congestion. Her liver was of average size, but it had evidence of fatty deposits. In addition, both of her kidneys appeared healthy and of normal size. Lastly, Jenkins noted that he found an undigested small blue pill in the woman's stomach, a pill that Kramer already identified as oxycodone.

Next, Kramer turned his focus to the draft toxicology report. The four-page report was full of numbers and laboratory findings that to a layperson would have appeared as a host of meaningless information with no apparent relevance. However, to an experienced forensic toxicologist like himself, the toxicology report, along with the findings of the autopsy, provided Kramer the needed information on which to base an opinion on the likely cause of the woman's death.

As in the autopsy report, the top-right corner of the toxicology report was stamped DRAFT in big letters. In the Case Information section, the name of the woman was listed as Unknown, and the Cause and Manner of Death were identified as pending. The only conclusive information in this section of the report was the sex (female) and race (white) of the deceased person.

The next section of the report, below the Case Information section, was where the laboratory findings were reported. It was here that results of the analysis for drugs of abuse were presented and where Kramer now focused his attention.

Identification and quantification of drugs of abuse in blood, including opioids, such as morphine and oxycodone; amphetamines; acetaminophen, also known as Tylenol; barbiturates, a class of sedative drugs; benzodiazepines; phencyclidine, known on the street as PCP; salicylates; tricyclic antidepressants; cannabinoids, the active ingredients in marijuana; cocaine; methadone; and alcohol is a time-consuming, multistep process. First, a screening method is used to identify whether the drugs are present in blood. Then, a gas chromatography/ mass spectrometry methodology, also known as GC/ MS, is used to confirm and quantify the drugs that were identified by the screening method. While the screening method is relatively inexpensive and rapid, it is fraught with false positives. On the other hand, GC/MS is very specific with a very low rate of false positives but is expensive and time consuming.

The preliminary drug screen showed that except for opioids, cocaine, and alcohol, no other drugs were detected in the dead woman's blood. The GC/MS confirmatory test identified the opioid as oxycodone, a central nervous system depressant whose blood level, based on published information in *Baselt*, was within the range that would be expected after ingesting a 30 milligram oxycodone tablet.

Baselt is short for the book *Disposition of Toxic Drugs and Chemicals in Man* by Randall C. Baselt, PhD, a former director of the Chemical Toxicology Institute in Foster City, California. The book is considered the bible of toxicology information by forensic toxicologists at medical examiner's offices nationwide, who refer to it when rendering their opinions. It contains summaries of toxicology information on over 675 drugs and chemicals that were abstracted from the published scientific literature. Each drug or chemical has its own chapter that includes sections on occurrence and usage, blood concentrations, metabolism and excretion, toxicity, analysis, and references.

From the amount of cocaine that was measured in the woman's blood, Kramer concluded that it was consumed at Camp David shortly before she died. Besides its euphoric properties, cocaine also causes narrowing of the arteries and increased blood pressure and heart rate. These side effects of cocaine further increased the woman's risk for a heart attack and death. Adding fuel to the fire was the large amount of alcohol that was found in her blood, an amount that was more than three times the legal limit. Alcohol combines with cocaine in a chemical reaction that yields cocaethylene, a substance that, like cocaine, is toxic to the heart but whose effects last much longer than those of cocaine. Consuming cocaine, an illegal drug, was bad enough, but ingesting large amounts of alcohol along with cocaine was a deadly combination.

Based on all the information presented in the draft autopsy and toxicology reports, Kramer concluded that the most likely explanation for how the woman died was from the combined effects of cocaine, oxycodone, and alcohol on her heart that, along with her existing anatomical risk factors, formed a perfect storm resulting in her death.

Although Kramer now understood how the woman died, he still did not know why she died. However, he was sure of at least one person who must be involved in her death. He picked up the phone and dialed Baker's phone number.

"I figured out what caused the woman's death," he told Baker when he answered. "Now we need to find out why she died and who else was involved."

"I have a pretty good idea what the answer to at least one of those questions is." Baker already identified the body as that of Erica Brown. Kramer did not know what else he had up his sleeve.

"I am going to set up a meeting with the vice president for tomorrow morning at 10:00 a.m.," Kramer announced, "and I am going to have Dave Singleton attend. Obviously, I want you to be there also, and I want you to bring the sixth CD with you. We are going to play it for the vice president and watch his face. It should be very interesting to see his reaction."

"I am looking forward to it already." Baker relished the thought.

"And please make sure that Bob Bacardi is there also. We are finally going to get to the bottom of this mess, and I do not want any possible miscommunication. I want him to hear the whole sordid affair directly from the horse's mouth. Besides, we will need to make use of his prosecutorial experience."

Baker knew exactly what Kramer meant. "I will definitely be there," he replied, "and I will make sure that Bacardi is there too." And with that, he hung up the phone.

Chapter 33

ALTHOUGH THE VICE president's residence is at the US Naval Observatory, he has two offices. One is located in the West Wing of the White House and the other, a ceremonial office that is mainly used for meetings and press interviews, is at the Eisenhower Executive Office Building. Kramer arranged to hold the meeting in the vice president's working office in the Executive Office Building. Everybody was already there by the time he arrived. He hoped that they did not wait for him too long.

The vice president was seated at his desk with the flag of the United States standing stoically behind him, slightly to his left. To his right stood his chief of staff, a yes-man with a Republican haircut that was neatly trimmed. He had no facial hair, which was consistent with the clean appearance of the Republicans. He was ready to answer any question, provide any information, or perform any task that might be required should the vice president not be able to do so. In the center of the room was a CD player that was plugged into a TV monitor that Kramer arranged beforehand so they could watch the sixth CD that Baker brought with him.

Bob Bacardi was seated on the sofa with pen and pad in hand, ready to take notes. He was concerned that the meeting would get out of hand should the vice president be uncooperative. Morgan Baker sat next to Bacardi, but he required nearly half the sofa just to be comfortable. He was sweating more than usual, which was not unexpected considering the stress that he was under with this investigation.

Dave Singleton sat in a stuffed, cushioned chair opposite the sofa, looking very serious. Kramer took a seat next to him, ready to officiate the meeting as soon as the vice president signaled that he was ready.

The atmosphere in the room was solemn. Everybody had a serious expression on his face except for the vice president, who, every so often, would turn to his chief of staff and whisper something in his ear, after which they would both chuckle. Kramer could not imagine what was so amusing. The vice president's demeanor suggested that he was unaware of the meeting's agenda.

The official White House photographer was also there, capturing every moment for posterity. The click of the camera's shutter could be heard breaking the silence as he roamed the perimeter of the room, looking for an interesting shot or the best angle to photograph. He was unconcerned about the meeting's agenda or its possible political ramifications. His only interest was to capture the expressions of the participants and the mood of the meeting for historical preservation. It would be many years before his photos would be reviewed by historians for their nuance and meaning about what was about to occur.

When the vice president finally motioned for the meeting to begin, Kramer rose from his chair and faced the vice president. "Mr. Vice President, thank you so much for providing us some time in your busy schedule on such short notice. We—"

"Let's cut to the chase," the vice president interrupted Kramer. He turned to his chief of staff. "Do you know what this meeting is all about?"

The chief of staff had an amused expression on his face and shrugged. Like a good puppy, he stood there at his master's beck and call.

"Except for that big fella over there"—Bunting pointed to Baker—"I know everybody here, so why don't you just introduce him and then let's move on?" He was anxious to begin. Kramer thought that Bunting must be late for an important date.

"This is Mr. Morgan Baker, Mr. Vice President. He is a private investigator from Louisiana." Kramer hoped to move slowly through the discussion so as not to alarm the vice president.

"A private investigator?" Bunting's expression dramatically changed. "Why is he here? Who hired a private investigator?" He looked around the room, but no one took him up on the challenge to respond. "I hope it doesn't cost the government any money." He turned to his chief of staff and chuckled again. "We have no slush fund for this sort of thing, do we?" Like a good yes-man, his chief of staff joined the vice president and laughed.

"The attorney general did, sir." It was Bob Bacardi who chimed in from the sofa, annoyed that Bunting was questioning his authority. "She hired Mr. Baker," he added, waited a bit, then added, "sir."

"Oh, I see. This must be important." Bunting looked down at some papers on his desk, rearranged them, and added, "Do I need to get my lawyer down here?" He looked at Bacardi, who did not flinch.

"We would like to keep this informal, Mr. Vice President, if it is all right with you." Bacardi anticipated that Bunting would wish to have his attorney present if he thought that he was being threatened in any way, so he received approval from the attorney general beforehand to keep the meeting informal.

Bunting looked around the room and saw that everybody was very serious and unnerved. He looked toward his chief of staff but saw nothing in his face that indicated what he should do next. "It is fine with me, if that is how you want to play it," he said and sat back in his chair, put his hands behind his head, and put his feet up on the desk. "Let's get on with it then."

Bunting has no inkling of what is about to transpire, Kramer thought. He didn't care. If he didn't know now, he soon would. "I would like you all to watch a CD that we obtained of part of the festivities on the evening of July fourth," Kramer began. "It is only thirty minutes long and was taken by one of the surveillance cameras on the street corner facing the East Gate of the White House." He motioned to Baker, who, with much difficulty, rose from the sofa and began fiddling with the CD player. At the same time, Bacardi pulled down the shades on all the windows and turned off all the lights in the room except for one that was dimly lit on the vice president's desk.

When he finished, he rushed to his seat so as not to miss any of the video and to watch it undisturbed.

After placing the CD into the CD player, Baker looked over to Kramer. "Ready?" Kramer nodded, and Baker pressed the Play button on the remote and went back to his seat. Six pairs of eyes were now glued to the TV monitor as the video began to roll.

Besides Baker and Kramer, no one in the room knew what they were about to see, but at the same time, no one wanted to miss anything that the video would reveal. Even Bunting stopped reclining and sat with his elbows on the desk, his head comfortably resting in his hands, and his eyes looking straight ahead at the monitor. *He is not chuckling now*, Kramer thought.

Images of the guests to the Fourth of July celebration could be seen exiting the White House and walking toward the East Gate of the White House. Buses were there, waiting to take them to Camp David. Occasionally, someone in the room would recognize one of the invited guests and would point toward the TV screen with pride. Here was Tewkesbury looking very uncomfortable in his tuxedo. There was Slocum looking presidential as he led his wife along the sidewalk.

Singleton concentrated on the TV monitor, hoping not to miss the point Kramer was trying to make. Kramer forewarned him to pay close attention, but so far, he did not see anything suspicious or incriminating.

They were now nearly at the point where the sound of the cannons exploding would be heard as the National Symphony Orchestra played Tchaikovsky's *Overture of 1812.* Bunting loved the *Overture* not only because it was beautiful music but because it was composed by Tchaikovsky, an openly gay man who was ahead of his time and who also composed music for the great ballets of *Sleeping Beauty, Swan Lake*, and *The Nutcracker.* As he listened, Bunting closed his eyes and relived the moment when he last heard the *Overture* on the evening of the Fourth of July.

The loud explosions of the cannons filled the room. If anyone was dozing off, they were very much awake now. Baker turned up the volume as soon as the cannons sounded so that everybody would pay closer attention when the moment they were waiting for finally arrived.

"Morgan, please put it on slow motion now," Kramer implored. It was the first time he called Baker by his first name, a sign that their professional relationship became close. Baker pressed the Slow Motion button on the remote. Figures on the screen moved slowly, their heads turning toward the White House to better hear the cannons and view the resounding fireworks. Bunting saw Jennifer Sweet at the front of the line; she was ready to board the first bus, and his eyes lit up at the sight of her. He was sorry that he broke off their relationship, but he promised the president that he would, and he always kept his promises.

"Morgan, please hit the Pause button now. I want you all to pay close attention to what you are about to see." Kramer jumped out of his seat. Everybody in the room moved to the edge of his seat, as if to get a better view of the TV screen, but there was no need to do that. They were only five to eight feet from the monitor, and each had an optimum viewing lane. Bacardi uncrossed his legs, ready to pounce up, if necessary. All eyes focused on the TV screen. Baker pressed the Slow Motion button again, and the images moved one frame at a time. Jennifer Sweet could be seen at the front of the line, ready to board the bus. Off to her right and hiding from view, a man appeared with a woman walking closely behind him. Unexpectedly, the man grabbed Sweet's right arm, and in one quick motion, pulled her to the side and to a waiting car, thereby allowing the woman who was trailing behind him to come into view.

"Quick, stop the video," Kramer shouted at Baker, who immediately complied. The video stopped at the moment when the woman's head could be easily seen. They could see that she bore a strong resemblance to Jennifer Sweet. Like Sweet, the woman wore a powder-blue gown with a fabric sash over her right shoulder, and like Sweet's, her blond hair was in an updo. She had long dangling earrings that Kramer and Baker recognized. In the darkness, the woman was a spitting image of Jennifer Sweet.

"Go ahead, and start the video again but in slow motion."

They saw the woman take Sweet's place in line and board the bus. The switch was so quick and sudden that no one in the procession saw it happen or suspected that anything was amiss. It was brilliantly planned, a switch of an impostor for an invited guest who was not seen or suspected by anyone but, thankfully, was captured by a police surveillance camera remotely placed at a street intersection.

And when the fireworks finally ended and the cannons and the orchestra were no longer heard, all the guests to the Fourth of July celebration turned their heads again toward the waiting buses and resumed their forward motion, oblivious of the dastardly deed that just occurred.

Everybody in the room was aghast and in total shock by what they viewed on the TV monitor. Bacardi's jaw dropped. Singleton was visibly shaken. Bunting sat forward in his chair, his face white as a ghost as blood rushed from his face down to his knees. Baker pressed the Stop button on the remote. There was no need to see anything else. Everybody understood that they saw a terrible thing that would not resonate well. It was obvious that the vice president was implicated in the switch, and it was time for him to provide a full explanation. Bacardi was the perfect person to get answers from the vice president. He rose from the couch and approached Bunting, thinking about how he should begin his questioning of the vice president.

As an attorney and a representative of the Justice Department, Bacardi had the knowledge, expertise, and political power to interrogate the vice president. He was not a special assistant to the attorney general because of his good looks. He proved his mettle on several occasions, and this was another such occasion in which his prosecutorial expertise was needed. "Mr. Vice President," he began, "as I mentioned earlier, we would like to handle this matter quietly and informally. The attorney general already gave her approval. She is not interested in putting the country through another Watergate. We are asking for your full and unconditional cooperation to help us get to the bottom of this sordid affair, including providing answers that would help us understand how the woman died at Camp David. We want your help, Mr. Vice President. Help us resolve many of the questions that still remain. We would like to put this whole incident behind us and are expecting your help and cooperation to do so. Are you willing to do that, Mr. Vice President?"

Bunting was a lawyer himself, and he considered the consequences of answering Bacardi's questions. Bacardi thought that Bunting was taking much too long to respond. *If he is worried about his political future,* Bacardi thought, *he better not. He would be extremely lucky to have any future at all by the time I am through with him.* He confronted the vice president again. "I should mention, Mr. Vice President, that if you are unwilling to give us your full cooperation, I have two Federal marshals waiting outside the door who are ready to escort you at my command."

"Of course I will cooperate, Mr. Bacardi." Bunting did not wait too long to respond. "Why wouldn't I?" he said snidely.

"Good. Let's begin."

Bacardi was mindful that he was about to interrogate the vice president of the United States. But there were many questions for which Bunting hopefully had the answers. It was Bunting who could shed light on what exactly happened at the White House–sponsored Fourth of July celebration that led to the woman's death at Camp David.

"Mr. Vice President," Bacardi began, "as I understand it, your guest for the celebration weekend was Ms.

Jennifer Sweet, true?" to which Bunting nodded. "Please tell me all about that."

"Well, there is not much to tell, really. I invited Ms. Sweet some time earlier to be my date for the event. I suppose she came to the White House through the East Gate and showed her credentials, just like everybody else did. She was there during the cocktail hour and dinner, and we watched most of the fireworks together before she was called to board the bus."

"Tell me about the evening. Did anything unusual happen between you two that evening?" *Interrogating well is like building a spiderweb. You start around the edges then slowly make your way toward the main point of concern when,* wham! *You hit the suspect with everything you have.*

"Yes, we had a good time together for most of the evening. She seemed to really enjoy herself. But sometime later, when we were watching the fireworks in the Rose Garden, we had an argument, after which I broke off our relationship." Bunting did not want to reveal too much to Bacardi.

"Oh? What did you argue about? Why did you break off the relationship?"

"After the photo appeared in the papers, you know, the one that was taken in Ohio, I promised the president that I would break off the relationship. Since I already

263

invited Ms. Sweet to the event, we attended together as planned. But while watching the fireworks, I made up an argument about some nonsense, and we broke up. She was devastated, of course, for which I am deeply sorry. But I promised the president that I would break it off, and I did. I always keep my promises. I think it was for the best."

Bacardi thought about that for a moment. "Did you intend for Ms. Sweet to get on the bus and go to Camp David?"

Bunting was reluctant to answer the question. If he did, there would be further questioning that he would find even more difficult to answer, so he just did not want to go there. But Bacardi was persistent. "Let me remind you, Mr. Vice President, that we expect your full and unconditional cooperation in this matter."

Eventually, Bunting replied. "No, I did not intend for Ms. Sweet to get on the bus to Camp David."

"And why not? Why was that?" Bacardi was like a dog chewing on a bone. He was not going to let go until he got the answers he was seeking.

"Because there was no way that Ms. Sweet was going to be going to Camp David."

"And why was that?" Bacardi persisted. He could play this game as long as anyone. He needed the vice president to be more forthcoming.

Bunting was in a bind. He was reluctant to provide any further details, but he knew that he could not skirt the question any longer. Bacardi was not going to stop until he was satisfied that he got the complete answer to his question.

"It was Tewkesbury," Bunting finally blurted out. "He made me do it. He thought things were going too well for the president with her reelection and that Slocum was losing badly in the polls. He wanted to embarrass the administration by having an impostor attend the event instead of Ms. Sweet so Slocum could have a chance of winning. He forced me to feign an argument with Ms. Sweet so she would be upset and would decide not to go to Camp David. At that time, an impostor would go in her place. But Ms. Sweet did not do what Tewkesbury expected. She planned to board the bus to Camp David anyway. That would have thwarted Tewkesbury's plan completely, so he had one of his men forcibly prevent Ms. Sweet from boarding. They then substituted someone else who boarded the bus in her place."

The vice president was in a tizzy and began to lose his composure. Bacardi looked around the room to see what effect Bunting's remarks were having on the people assembled there. He saw Singleton leaning forward in his chair, and he held his eyes for what seemed like a very long time. The president's lawyer could not believe what he was hearing. Here was the vice president purposely shafting the president for political gain after everything that she did for him. But why? What did Tewkesbury have over Bunting that forced the vice president to give in to such a scheme?

"And that someone who boarded the bus instead of Ms. Sweet was?" Bacardi looked over to Baker, who rose again.

"Erica Brown, a forty-three-year-old transgender from Washington, DC," was Baker's reply, after which he sat down again.

"I did not know she was a transgender. I did not know anything about that!" Bunting looked around the room for support but did not find any. "I did not know that Tewkesbury planned to have a transgender there. He only told me to make sure that Ms. Sweet would not go to Camp David. I did not know what his plan was after that," he pleaded.

Looking again at Singleton with his back to Bunting, Bacardi continued. "Apparently, Tewkesbury planned it for a very long time because he knew exactly what Jennifer Sweet was going to wear that night, right down to her earrings. He also knew how she was going to do her hair, what lipstick she was going to wear, what her makeup would look like, et cetera, et cetera, et cetera." He turned to face Bunting. "Tewkesbury had you buy the powder-blue Christian Dior gown and the long David Yurman dangling earrings for Ms. Sweet to wear that night because he bought the same outfit and earrings for Ms. Brown to wear that night, right?" to which Bunting nodded.

"You strongly advised Ms. Sweet," Bacardi continued, "to wear her hair in an updo that night because Tewkesbury told you to do so. Isn't that right?" Again, Bunting nodded.

"Tewkesbury planned to have Ms. Brown go to Camp David instead of Ms. Sweet, and he needed your help to ensure that the two women resembled each other so that no one would suspect that a switch was made. Isn't that right, Mr. Vice President?" Bacardi was shouting now, his gaze piercing the vice president, whose lips were quivering as his composure began to deteriorate.

"Yes, it is," the vice president replied, his voice breaking. "Tewkesbury made me do it."

"But why?" It was Singleton. "Why did you do it? Just tell me. I don't understand?" He was almost in tears.

"We will get to that in a minute, Mr. Singleton, but before we do, let me ask the vice president a few more questions that will further clarify the matter," Bacardi interjected before the vice president could respond.

"Mr. Vice President," Bacardi began again, "as we saw earlier, Ms. Brown boarded the bus instead of Ms.

Sweet. She is the one who went to Camp David and not Ms. Sweet. That explains why Ms. Kendall was able to confirm that two hundred people boarded the buses, the same number of people who were invited to the event and who were at the White House reception and dinner. Now tell me, what happened later that night at Camp David between you and Ms. Brown? Surely you interacted that evening."

"Well, nothing really happened," Bunting said, but Bacardi stopped him short.

"Now, come on, Mr. Vice President. Don't give me that. Surely, something happened that night that led to her death. Don't keep us in suspense. Get on with it. Get it out there, Mr. Vice President." Bacardi was losing his temper.

"We were together most of the evening, but we tried our best to keep away from the others so they would not notice that Ms. Brown was an impostor. I didn't know she was a transgender. I swear it. You must believe me." He looked around at the others in the room, but he was not getting any sympathy from anybody. "Ms. Sweet was assigned her own separate room, so Ms. Brown occupied that room in her place. All was going smoothly, but at about one o'clock in the morning, there was a knock on my door. I was already in bed and in my briefs, but I got out of bed to see who it was that was knocking on my door at that time of the night. When I opened the door, Ms. Brown was standing there with one hand holding the doorframe and the other holding a glass of wine, smiling a sardonic smile."

"Were you alone before she knocked on the door? Were you alone in the room?" Bacardi asked.

"Well, no," the vice president replied. "I had a visitor, and I did not want to be disturbed. Ms. Brown stood at the doorway, and the door was partially open, so she looked over my shoulder and saw that someone was in my bed. I was surprised to see her at my doorstep at that time of night. I looked around and into the hallway to make sure that no one was in the corridor watching us. There was no one there. I asked her in a hushed voice, almost in a whisper, what she was doing there, and she responded, 'I just came to see if you wanted some company, but I see that you already have company.' Then, without warning, she pushed me aside, opened the door, and staggered into the room. I thought she was high."

"And what happened next?"

"Well, she walked in, or should I say, she weaved in. She really seemed high. She put down her wineglass on the coffee table and unzipped the back of her dress, letting it fall to the floor, and said, 'I guess we will just have to have a threesome, won't we?' Then she added, 'What do you call that? Ménage à trois?' The next thing I knew, she threw her head back, let out a loud, hearty laugh, and removed three hairpins from her head, disentangling her hair. With one shake of the head, her long blond tresses fell to her shoulders, framing her face with a golden hue. She was ready to party, whereas I was ready to go to bed."

"And what did you do?"

"I was standing there in my skivvies, dumbfounded, but she grabbed me with one hand round my neck and pulled me down, and we both fell on the bed. I tried to resist, but she held me tight, kissed me deeply, then switched partners and did it all over again."

Kramer looked at Baker, who looked back at him with total bewilderment. They were flabbergasted. They heard more than either one of them anticipated, and it was not pretty. Here was the vice president totally out of control. He was being manipulated by the campaign manager of the presumptive Republican candidate for president of the United States and having a rendezvous with an impostor.

Bacardi resumed his questioning. "And who was the other woman in the bed, Mr. Vice President, the one who was in the room before Ms. Brown appeared at your doorstep. Who was she?"

With pleading eyes, Bunting looked at Bacardi as if to say, "Please don't have me say it," but Bacardi would have none of that. He wanted every last bit of detail to be aired in the confines of the vice president's office. He asked again, "Who was she, Mr. Vice President? Who was the other woman in your bed?"

Bunting looked around the room and saw that all eyes were upon him. Singleton seemed depressed and tense in his seat, all air having gone out of his balloon. Kramer and Baker were looking down at their hands, completely in shock. Bacardi, while moving forward in his questioning, was taken aback by what he was hearing. Even Bunting's chief of staff stood there, having a difficult time believing everything that was taking place.

"It was not a she, Mr. Bacardi." Bunting inhaled deeply and took another long look around the room, hoping to see if anybody comprehended what he was about to say. "It was not a she at all," he repeated. "It was a he. It was John Worthing, the president's husband. He was the person in my bed that night." A loud gasp escaped from Singleton before he covered his mouth with the palm of his hand in total disbelief.

Kramer and Baker could not help themselves. "Oh no!" they said in unison. What they heard was totally unexpected. "Gevalt," Kramer added.

Bunting sat back in his chair, almost relieved that his secret was finally out. He was holding back for so long, and the burden became unbearable.

Waiting for what seemed like a very long time, although it was only a couple of minutes, Bacardi was still trying to digest everything that the vice president told him. He also wanted the others to compose themselves. Sure, they heard many unsavory things from the vice president today, including a story about Republican dirty tricks. But that was only one part of the story. They still had to find out how Ms. Brown died and who was responsible for her death. When they recomposed themselves, Bacardi returned to questioning the vice president.

"Let's get back to what happened in your room, Mr. Vice President, after Ms. Brown seduced the both of you. Tell me what happened next."

"She still had her glass of wine, so she continued drinking, and when she finished her glass, I took another bottle from the bar, and all three of us—me, Mr. Worthing, and Ms. Brown—sat on the floor, half naked, and finished off the bottle. We kept toasting each other over the next hour or so while Ms. Brown continued to laugh hysterically. She was having a really great time. She must have had at least seven glasses of wine when all of a sudden, a frightened look came across her face as she held her chest and keeled over. It was very sudden and a complete surprise to all of us."

"You mean to you and Mr. Worthing, right? There was nobody else in the room except the two of you and Ms. Brown, right?" Bacardi interjected.

"Yes, John and I were caught completely off guard. We didn't know what to do next. I checked Ms. Brown's pulse, but there was none. We placed a small mirror near her nose, but it was no use. She was not breathing. We eventually decided that she was dead."

"What happened then?"

"Well, we couldn't leave her in my room where she would be found the next morning, now could we?" Bunting's eyes were large. "I told John to keep quiet as I peeked out the door to check to see if there was anybody there. Not seeing anyone, John picked up Ms. Brown's feet while I picked up her upper body and purse, and together we lifted her out the door. After a quick right turn, we exited the building. As we stood outside the door, I saw an area across the way that had a huge oak tree with large branches that provided maximum shade. It was a perfect place to put the body because the area was completely dark with no illumination from the overhead strobe light. The bulb appeared to be broken. We sprinted across the path, making sure we did not drop or drag the body on the ground. When we arrived at the tree, we placed the body in the darkest area where there was maximum shade. It was three in the morning by the time we returned to the room. We agreed to never talk about it again, and we haven't."

"Until now, right?" Bacardi asked, to which the vice president again nodded.

Bacardi thought, *What happens now? Where do we go from here? There is no way that the country will withstand such a sordid affair, and the attorney general certainly will not sanction it.*

"Excuse me, Mr. Bacardi," Kramer said as he stood up. "May I say something? I would like to add some information, if it is all right." Bacardi raised his eyebrows as if questioning what Kramer could possibly add to the conversation, but he let him take the floor.

"I cannot say anything about the relationship between the vice president and the president's husband, John Worthing. That is a personal matter that is best sorted out by the president herself. As for Tewkesbury's dirty-tricks campaign, in my opinion, that is best dealt with by Mr. Dearling, the president's campaign manager, and Mr. Singleton, the president's attorney. However, as far as Ms. Brown is concerned, she was a real person who was placed in an unfortunate position, in part because of her own choosing but mostly because Mr. Tewkesbury placed her into what turned out to be a life-threatening situation for political gain. It was more than unfortunate. It was tragic. As for the cause of her death, that is something that I am very qualified to talk about since I have some expertise in pharmacology and toxicology and analyzing cause of death. Now, I have reviewed the autopsy and toxicology reports and the relevant scientific literature and concluded that Ms. Brown had an undiagnosed heart condition. Unfortunately, she consumed oxycodone, a narcotic medication, and cocaine, an illegal drug, while at Camp David, sometime before she visited the vice president's room. Also, she ingested a substantial amount of alcohol over a relatively short time in the company of the vice president and Mr. Worthing. The combination of oxycodone, alcohol, and cocaine is very toxic to the heart and could be deadly, especially in a person having an enlarged heart and suffering from coronary atherosclerosis, as Ms. Brown was. Taking all this information together, it is my professional opinion within a reasonable degree of scientific certainty that Ms. Brown died from a heart attack that was caused by the combined effects of cocaine, oxycodone, and alcohol and her existing risk factors for a cardiac-related event. Her death, therefore, was accidental."

Bacardi listened to Kramer's explanation and was impressed. *Kramer certainly knows his stuff*, he thought. Bacardi now not only knew how Ms. Brown died but also why she died. It was nobody's fault, yet it was everybody's fault. There was plenty of blame to go around for everyone to share—the vice president, the president's husband, and the Republican campaign manager, Mr. Tewkesbury. As tragic as Ms. Brown's death was, there was no criminal case to be made. Sure, entering Camp David without a proper security check and bringing cocaine to the camp was a security breach that would be handled appropriately, and those responsible would be reprimanded accordingly. But as for a criminal case, there was no homicide here, only an accidental death that should never have happened. The only winners in this whole mess were the American people. They would see security at Camp David improved and an election in November that would be more fair, thanks in large part to the tragic death of Erica Brown, a transgender. Unfortunately, however, her contribution to democracy would never appear in the history books.

Chapter 34

SINGLETON CONFRONTED TEWKESBURY with the news that Bunting would be resigning at the end of his current term. There was no need for Tewkesbury to feign surprise. He suspected as much, based on Singleton's expression. It was obvious that the president's lawyer knew about the dirty tricks that Tewkesbury initiated at the Fourth of July celebration event. There was not much he could say to Singleton to make amends.

"But why did you do it?" Singleton asked. "What did you have to gain?"

"Slocum was losing badly in the polls, and we had to do something. I didn't expect it to turn out the way it did. I certainly did not plan that Ms. Brown would die. That was very unfortunate."

"Unfortunate? Is that what you call it? Unfortunate?" Singleton was incredulous. "No death is unfortunate, especially not the death of Erica Brown. Every life is precious. It was tragic, that is what it was. It was tragic and totally unnecessary." Singleton could not contain himself. "I am sure that Ms. Brown thought that she was participating in a simple prank, but instead, she wound up dead, and it was all your fault."

"My fault? My fault? I didn't know she had a heart condition or used cocaine. I certainly didn't approve her bringing cocaine to Camp David. That was all her doing. And besides, what about all the drinking? Was that my fault also?"

Singleton was disgusted. "You put her in a precarious, unwinnable situation. You should have ensured her safety, or better yet, you should not have done this dirty trick at all. Her death lies squarely at your feet and on your conscience, and you will have to live with it for the rest of your life."

There was nothing further for Tewkesbury to say. What could he say? Singleton was right, of course, but the deed was done, and there was no way to turn the clock back.

"I expect you to resign," Singleton advised Tewkesbury. "I prefer not to go to the press, but I will if you force my hand. The country had enough of Watergate-type politics, and it will not stand for a repeat performance."

Polling was what Tewkesbury was all about, not campaign management. He tried being a campaign manager, but it obviously did not suit him. He would go back to his ranch, take a nice, long vacation, and fade from view. Let others carry the ball to the finish line.

"I will," he replied. "I will tell Slocum, and I will depart forever. Politics is not my cup of tea anyway."

"Before I go, however, tell me one thing. What did you have over Bunting that he was willing to participate in this fiasco? How did you manage to convince him to assist you with this plan?"

"He didn't remember me at first, but we were in college together and belonged to the same fraternity," Tewkesbury said as he shuffled his feet and shrugged his shoulders. "I always resented him because he followed his dream into politics while I joined the army and nearly got myself killed in Afghanistan, all to keep guys like him safe at home. If it was not for Slocum, I would not be here today. Anyway, back in college, Bunting liked the ladies, but one day, I accidentally caught him having sex with a man."

"You did?"

"Yeah, I accidentally opened the door to his room and found him having sex with a man. I was extremely surprised to see this, and he was shocked to see me as well, but I never said anything about the incident to anyone. That was many years ago, and it was nearly forgotten until I became Slocum's campaign manager, and it all surfaced again. Bunting became paranoid and tried to have me fired. I knew more about paranoia and depression than he did, so I reminded him of his earlier exploits. He tried to reassure me that it was a one-time thing that he did in his youth and that he had not done that sort of thing since then. I did not believe him, and apparently I was right to doubt him. When I cooked up the plan to have Brown switch with Sweet, I needed Bunting's help so I hinted that if I didn't get his assistance, I would expose him. He agreed to assist."

"Wow! That is some fucking story." Singleton could not believe that he said that, but he had a very trying day. He was a very proper, straight-as-an-arrow, professional man who never uttered a cuss word. Today, he heard just about everything, and he had to release all the venom that was within him.

"I don't want to know any more," he said. "Just get yourself out of Washington, and the sooner the better. You make me sick!" He turned and walked away.

Singleton's next stop was at the White House. He met with President Worthing and told her that the mystery of the death of the woman at Camp David was solved and that her vice president was implicated in the death and was resigning at the end of his term. Singleton expected Worthing to be shocked by the news, but she took it in stride. There was not much more she could do with Bunting. Singleton warned her that Bunting was unpredictable, and he was right. It was time for him to go.

"And your husband is gay," Singleton added and advised her to consider divorcing John Worthing after the November election. He didn't expect to get the reaction he received from the president after hearing the news about her husband. She bent over with laughter the likes of which he never heard from her before. When she finally composed herself, she inquired, "Is that all? Is that all?" she kept repeating. "I knew he was gay all along. That's why I married him." She let out a big belly laugh again and walked about the room in circles. Singleton didn't understand and did not know what to say. His face was one big question mark. He hoped that no one would enter the Oval Office and see the president in such a state.

"I am also gay!" she finally exclaimed when she stopped laughing. "Can't you tell, after knowing me all these years? Couldn't you tell?" Then, she laughed hysterically. Singleton left the Oval Office dumbfounded, leaving the door wide open as the sound of the president's maniacal laughter followed him in his wake.

Chapter 35

THE DEMOCRATIC NATIONAL Convention was in full swing in Colorado by the second week of September. Like their Republican counterparts, the Democrats were prone to lengthy, boring speeches that went nowhere. Although there was no doubt that Jessica Worthing would be nominated for president by her party, essentially unopposed, her reelection to the post was not assured now that Vice President Bunting took his name off the ballot. It seems he unexpectedly developed an unspecified illness for which medical attention was required and that precluded his being Worthing's running mate in the upcoming November election. That brought much needed suspense to the convention that, until Bunting's announcement, appeared to be a mere formality. Worthing's selection of a new vice presidential running mate was just the spark that was needed to keep the nation tuned to CNN until the final moments of the convention.

Jennifer Sweet called Kramer earlier in the week and told him that she would be having another layover in DC. Kramer loved the idea of a layover and thought that whoever invented the word was a genius. He suggested that they skip dinner and meet at his penthouse condominium apartment in Chevy Chase, Maryland, because he wanted to take full advantage of the opportunity to lay over her, assuming she had no objections. She giggled and agreed to meet him on the last night of the convention.

As previously, Kramer and Sweet made love to the background sounds of speeches from the convention. Kramer was grateful for the chance to lie over Sweet, thanks to American Airlines's policy of resting its personnel before their next flight. Sweet being sweet on Kramer made sure that he was satisfied with her performance, which he undoubtedly was. Eventually, they reversed positions so that Sweet lay on top of Kramer. This provided him the opportunity to enjoy her nipples and feel the smoothness of her buttocks while, at the same time, watch Jessica Worthing announce her pick for vice president. It was a win-win position that

Kramer thought was brilliant. He wondered why he did not think of it earlier when they first made love during the Republican National Convention. Was it because he was biased toward the Democrats or simply because he wanted to try a new position? He did not know the answer or care to know. Sweet did not give him much time to think about it because she kept exploring his body from overhead, sometimes obscuring his view of the television screen.

"Am I glad that I had this layover," Sweet said between kisses as her soft hands roamed Kramer's body, searching to see if he was aroused. He was.

"So am I," he answered as he strained to see the telecast from his partially obscured vantage point. "We should lay over more often," he added, to which Sweet let out a small giggle, which was so flirtatious that he nearly climaxed right then and there.

They kissed and hugged and then kissed some more, and all the while, Kramer kept his ears partially tuned to the convention, anxious to hear Worthing announce her selection for vice president. Sweet, on the other hand, found nooks and crannies on Kramer's body that he never knew existed. She made the most of them, touching here with soft, manicured hands or licking there with her warm, moist tongue. So magical and sensual was

Sweet's expertise in the art of lovemaking that Kramer was barely able to keep himself together.

"Go ahead and let go," Sweet said, noticing Kramer tense up. "Don't worry. I will be here all night." She stretched those final two words as she nibbled on his ear and massaged his manhood. Kramer tried to think about something mundane, like the weather, lest he explode.

Finally taking the podium to loud applause, Jessica Worthing smiled, waved, and nodded. *"My fellow Democrats"*—there was thunderous applause—*"I accept your nomination for president of the United States."*

"It is almost over," Kramer said as he tenderly kissed Sweet.

She raised her head in shock. "What?" She was almost crying. "Are you telling me we are almost through?" Her face took on a hurt expression.

"No, no, my sweet Sweet." Kramer tried to reassure her as he kissed her some more. "I was talking about the convention. It is almost over, at least for another four years." He lowered his hand past her garden, searching for her flower. Finding it, he inserted his middle finger and massaged the sentry standing at his post. Sweet relaxed, the worry lines fading from her face. Ecstasy overtook her. When she was done moaning and groaning, she whispered in his ear, "You had me worried." Then, almost as an afterthought, she added, "You are so amazing, Dr. Kramer," to which he replied, "I know."

Kramer loved Jennifer Sweet's smile. He remembered the first time she smiled at him on the flight from New Orleans to DC about two months earlier. He was not the same since. Her exquisite vision haunted him until they reconnected on the last night of the Republican National Convention. Now, here they were, connecting again, only this time, it was on the last night of the Democratic National Convention. "Isn't politically correct wonderful? Equal opportunity for all." His laughter was so contagious that Sweet could not help but join in.

"I want to introduce to you the next vice president"— Jessica Worthing was nearly finished with her lengthy acceptance speech. She summarized her achievements over the previous two years in fifty-five minutes and was ready to announce her selection of a running mate. The silence on the convention floor was a strong contrast to the anticipated enthusiastic roar that would follow her announcement. All the delegates held their breath and waited patiently for the name of the lucky person to be announced and for his or her picture to be displayed on the jumbotron—*"of the United States."* At that precise moment, a moment when the nation and the world expected to hear the name and to see the face

of the Democratic vice presidential nominee, the hall went dark, the microphone stopped working, and the jumbotron became a mere blank advertising display as a total blackout swept the nation's capital and its surrounding suburbs.

"Oh no!" Kramer nearly pushed Sweet off the bed. "Damn it! What the hell happened?" He jumped out of bed and looked out the window but saw only darkness. The blackout permeated throughout the neighborhood, and there was only blackness in DC, Maryland, and Virginia. "You may as well come back to bed," Sweet said as she pulled the cover to the side, waiting for Kramer to return to her embrace. "There is nothing that you can do anyway."

Kramer's frustration was understandable. He very much looked forward to finding out who Worthing picked as her vice presidential running mate. Now, he would have to wait until the following morning for the news. Sweet beckoned him to return to bed. He did. She, in turn, resumed her place on top of Kramer and purred in his ear, "Did you ever solve the mystery of the death of the woman at Camp David?"

"I shouldn't tell you, and besides, you wouldn't believe me even if I told you." Kramer smiled as he borrowed a line Sweet uttered previously when they made love to the sounds of the Republican National Convention.

"Try me," she said and gave him a soft love tap on the shoulder, "I wouldn't tell anybody. I promise."

"All right, I will. Remember the woman who took your place on the bus that night and went to Camp David instead of you?"

She nodded her head. "How can I forget?"

"Well, she was a transgender."

"No way!" Sweet said in amazement.

"And the body that they found at Camp David," he continued, "was the body of the same transgender who replaced you on the bus."

"Oh my god!" Sweet exclaimed. "This is getting very interesting. Did they identify the body by name?"

"Yes," Kramer responded. "Her name was Erica Brown. She was forty-three years old and a well-known transgender in Washington, DC."

"Anything else?" Sweet was all ears now.

"Well, the woman died from an undiagnosed heart condition that was aggravated by cocaine and oxycodone and by drinking lots of alcohol with the vice president and the president's husband, John Worthing. Bunting and John Worthing tried to cover up her death by placing the body under a big oak tree so it would not be found in the vice president's room the following morning."

"I don't know if I can take any more of this." Sweet gasped for air. "Is there much more?"

"Only one more thing." Kramer left the best for last. "Bunting and Worthing were lovers."

"Heaven help us," Sweet proclaimed. "What is the country coming to?" She paused then quickly added, "Not that there is anything wrong with that!" They both broke into uncontrollable laughter. Kramer kicked the blanket off the bed, wrapped his arms and legs around Sweet, and pulled her closer, kissing her long and hard. *She may be a shiksa*, he thought as he kissed her, *but she kisses like a Jewish princess.* His kissing would not be the last long and hard thing Jennifer Sweet would feel that night.

Epilogue

THE GAP BETWEEN the Democratic and Republican slates for president and vice president tightened considerably by November. Jessica Worthing selected a Democrat to be her running mate, and most polls still had her ahead of her Republican challenger by four to six points, which was within the margin of error. However, Slocum and Jackson were making inroads in Southern States, and with one week left before the general election, they were confident that they could surpass Worthing in the important state of Ohio. People predicted that it would be a very close election.

No one seemed to care that Eric Bunting faded from view, presumably for medical attention, and that John

Worthing was nowhere to be seen either. It was a new day, and people were absorbed in the football playoffs and turned their attention to other events. The whereabouts of Bunting and John Worthing was the last thing on most people's mind.

Baker returned to Louisiana but promised to stay in touch with Kramer, hoping that they would work together on future cases. Their relationship had flourished. Kramer was sure that he would need Baker's expertise in some of his upcoming cases. As for Jennifer Sweet, she returned to her job as a flight attendant for American Airlines, but her relationship with Kramer did not wane. They enjoyed each other's company whenever their schedules coincided.

On election night, Kramer did not watch the election returns. He was already involved in a new case that required his undivided attention. The death of the woman at Camp David was a tragic event, but his new medical malpractice case in which a man died at a local hospital bordered on a possible homicide. He had much more work to do before he could render an opinion on the likely cause of the man's death.

CPSIA information can be obtained
at www.ICGtesting.com
Printed in the USA
BVOW03s1850151116
467938BV00001B/48/P